)o you want to buy a copy
of this (or almost any) book?
The library will "special order"
: for you. Ask for details.

MY UNDERRATED YEAR

My Underrated Year

Randy Powell

A Sunburst Book
Farrar, Straus and Giroux

To my mother and father, with love

MY UNDERRATED YEAR

1

MIKE BROCK and I worked all summer at the Clover Park Golf and Tennis Club, giving tennis lessons. He taught the "Teens"—mostly thirteen-year-old girls who swooned over him—while I got stuck with the "Nine-and-Unders," little runts who spent most of the time trying to bombard me with tennis balls. After the lessons, if Brock felt like it, he and I would play a match. He was a senior at Hillside High School, number one on Hillside's tennis team and a star at football and basketball. I was a sophomore at Clover Park. I'd been number three on my tennis team the year before, and since the number one and two players had both graduated, it looked like I'd be number one that spring. I'd have to play Brock when our teams met, so I felt lucky just to be on the same court with him that summer, even though he beat me every time.

But the last day of vacation I did something I'd never expected to do. I beat him, 5–7, 6–4, 6–4. When I shot

3

my serve by him for an ace on match point, he turned around and slammed his racquet against the chain-link fence. Then he walked over and shook hands with me.

On the way home from the club that day, as I pumped my bike up the hill to my house, I had visions of beating Brock in the league tournament. By the time I made it to the driveway, sweat was running down my face and stinging my eyes. I stopped and wiped my face with my shirttail. When I looked up, I saw Clay Brodie sitting on the front porch. He was wearing his dirty white football jersey, and his muddy football shoes were slung over his shoulder. Brodie's been my best friend since kindergarten.

"Where were you all day, Roger?" he asked.

We'd been having pre-season football workouts since the middle of August and our last one had been the day before, but that afternoon I'd missed a touch-football game at the high school.

"I got into a match with Brock," I said as I unlocked the front door. "I beat him."

Brodie followed me inside. When we got to the kitchen he stopped and faced me with that deadpan look of his, and even though I knew he didn't care anything about tennis, I thought for sure he was going to say something about me beating Brock. It was worth a comment, even from Brodie.

"I've got one word to say," he said.

"What's that?"

He waited a few seconds before saying it: "Varsity."

"What about it?" I said.

"What about it? I'll tell you what about it. It looks good for us, man. It looks better than good."

4

"Really?"

He still had that serious expression. "Kortum and Hiddleston told me a few things today."

Bob Kortum and Julian Hiddleston were the two captains of the varsity football team, both seniors. Kortum was a linebacker—probably the best in the state—and Hiddleston was our stud quarterback—Clover Park's version of Mike Brock.

"What did they say?" I asked.

"They said the coaches aren't real crazy about Hogness, even though he'll probably start at running back because he's a senior. But the coaches think he's too slow. They want somebody who's quick. Like you."

"The coaches said that?"

Brodie shrugged. "According to Kortum and Hiddleston. And they said I've got a good shot at varsity linebacker."

In our school, only three or four sophomores made varsity each year, and they were the guys who happened to be built like buses at the age of fifteen. The rest of us sophomores, especially the tall, lanky running backs like me, had to spend the year on junior varsity.

"You really think it looks good?" I asked.

"I think it looks damn good."

He opened the refrigerator and helped himself to the bottle of Gatorade that I always keep in there.

"So what was the game like today?" I asked.

I waited for him to finish guzzling. When he pulled the bottle away, he let out a breathless grunt, then said, "Not bad. We had enough for four teams. I was on Kortum's." He grabbed a doughnut and stuffed half of it into his mouth.

I hopped up on the kitchen counter, with my heels kicking against the drawers, and tossed my house keys up and down in my hand. I thought about making varsity. Things like making varsity football when you're only a sophomore just didn't happen to guys like me. As a junior, sure, because that's the typical thing. But not as a sophomore. No, something kept circling around in my head, something like, *Too good to be true...*

Brodie was still talking.

"Huh?" I said, looking up.

"I said he wasn't bad."

"Who?"

"The guy I just told you about."

"I wasn't listening."

"I noticed."

"Who were you talking about?"

"The new guy," Brodie said. "He's a sophomore. He just moved here. He isn't bad."

"At what?"

"Running back."

Something in my stomach kicked. *Too good to be true...*

"What was so great about him?" I asked.

"I didn't say he was great. I just said he was decent. Maybe a little better than decent."

"How can you tell in a touch-football game?"

"He had good moves. And a great stiff-arm, even in a touch-football game. And strong. One of those short chunky builds, you know, like a bowling ball. Not as fast as you, maybe, but Kortum was impressed."

"He was?"

"Yeah."

6

"What's the guy's name?"

"Mountain. I'll show him to you at school tomorrow."

After Brodie left, I went upstairs to my room and opened my closet door and looked at my football shoes. Something was still bothering me, still circling around in my head. I went to the window and looked out at the street. To my right, Brodie was on his way down the hill. To my left, the street continued up the hill, past another three houses, until it hit the vacant lots at the dead end. Above that was the bluff I had run every single evening that summer. It was a rough, steep two hundred feet to the top. You had to zigzag around big tufts of weeds and dig your feet into the deep sandy dirt. Halfway up, you felt your lungs burn and your legs tighten. It was pure agony. But when you got to the top, you could see the whole town of Clover Park. You felt like you deserved to relax, to just sit and think.

I went back to the closet and grabbed my football shoes.

When I got to the top, I bent over, panting and sweating. Pretty soon I could breathe again. After a while, my heartbeat was back to normal. I sat down with my back against a tree and grabbed a handful of pebbles and started tossing them at a tree farther down the slope. I thought about how I'd beaten Brock, and how he had come up to the net and shaken hands with me. I guess when guys like Brock do something like shake hands with you, it makes you feel pretty important. You feel like a Somebody instead of a Nobody.

I thought about Kortum and Hiddleston talking to

7

Brodie about me, saying I had a good shot at varsity. If I made it, Mom would flip. She really would. She understands what it means for a sophomore to make varsity for the Clover Park Loggers. She knows Clover Park football.

It would be nice to see her flip for a change. I think I'm kind of a disappointment to her. She probably wonders how she and my dad could have ended up with me. I mean, when they were in high school, they were both popular and they hung out with the cool people and went to dances and parties and that sort of thing. My dad played varsity football his junior and senior years, and my mom was a cheerleader. They got married right out of high school, and a while after that, I was born. Then my dad got a job at the lumber mill. About his third week there, he was riding a forklift up a ramp and the forklift tipped over and fell on him, and that was it for my dad.

Mom doesn't talk about him very much, but when she does, it's usually about their high school days, not about when they were married. I think she misses those days. She wishes I hung out with a "crowd" and brought kids home and had parties and went on dates. She wishes I'd meet some "cute girls." She thinks Brodie's weird because he's never had a girlfriend. Which means she thinks I'm weird, too.

I closed my eyes and pictured my favorite fantasy: playing tennis on a spring day with a beautiful girl. People would gather around to watch us; they'd wonder who I was, to be playing tennis with such a pretty, classy girl. That fantasy always made me feel good, but it always gave me a hollow feeling too, because it was only a fantasy, it wasn't real.

So I decided to concentrate on reality. This was a brand-new year, with a brand-new Roger Ottosen. A

Roger Ottosen who had a good shot at making varsity football, who was a sure thing for number one on the tennis team, who had a chance of beating Mike Brock and going to the league championships. What a year this could be.

Maybe the greatest year of my life.

2

I'VE ALWAYS HATED the first day of school. There's all
these new people walking around. There's always a bunch
of suntanned girls running up to each other and hugging
and talking about the exciting summer they had. It's
pretty depressing.

In our school there's this place called the Intersection. It's just that, a place where four different hallways
come together. Over on one side, next to the trophy display case, there's a lounge area where students can sit and
watch people walk by. Supposedly anybody can sit there,
but only the cool seniors do.

Kortum and Hiddleston and about six other senior
jocks were all there with their chairs tipped back against
the wall. Across town at Hillside, you could be sure Mike
Brock and his friends were doing exactly the same thing
in their own place reserved for cool people only. Brodie
and I just stood leaning against the wall. We were waiting
for the new guy, Mountain, to come along, so Brodie
could point him out to me.

The next thing you know, something pretty strange happened. This girl I'd never seen before came walking through the Intersection. A couple of seniors whistled at her. She had a dark suntan and thick brownish hair down to her shoulders. She was beautiful.

But that wasn't the strange part. The strange part was, she looked right at me, smiled and said, "Hi, Roger," and continued on down the hall.

"Who was that?" Brodie asked. "How does she know your name?"

I shook my head. "I don't know."

"Why would she say hello to you?"

"Thanks, Brodie." But I was wondering the same thing. "Maybe she's seen me at the club. Maybe she's got a little brother or sister who took lessons from me this summer."

"And the brother or sister told her your name," Brodie said, nodding. "And she saw you just now, and since she's new and you're the only person in Clover Park whose name she knows, she said hello to you. That explains it. Yeah, that makes sense."

We watched more people walk by.

"She hasn't found out you're a sophomore," he said after a while. "She hasn't found out who you are."

What he meant was, she hadn't found out what a jerk I was. But I reminded myself that this was a new year. She didn't know me. Wait till she found out I was going to make varsity football as a sophomore and be number one on the tennis team this spring. Maybe that didn't make me a Hiddleston or a Kortum or a Brock, but it made me a Somebody. *She* wouldn't know I'd been a Nobody all my life.

I was thinking about that, when suddenly there was

this big commotion down the hall in one of the locker bays. Some kid was getting himself slammed against the lockers. Even Hiddleston and Kortum and the other cool seniors took time out from tipping their chairs against the wall to stand up and see what was going on.

"It's Playchek," Brodie muttered with a disgusted look.

"Who's he got?" I asked.

"Some freshman. He's picking on a stupid little ninth-grader."

As soon as Kortum and Hiddleston and the rest saw that it was Byron Playchek, they sat down and went back to looking cool. People talked about what would happen if Bob Kortum and Byron Playchek ever got into a fight. Everybody said Kortum would win—of course Kortum would win. It was like believing that Good will beat Evil. Kortum stood for America, and Playchek stood for...I don't know, he stood for the Terrorists or something. But nobody would ever find out whether Kortum could beat Playchek, because Kortum and Playchek stayed clear of each other. So everybody said Kortum would beat Playchek, because deep down everybody was afraid that maybe Kortum *wouldn't* beat Playchek, and if that happened, anything could happen—America could get whipped by the Terrorists.

Playchek always wore a dirty sleeveless T-shirt that showed off his huge red arms. He was a fat pig, but man, was he strong. He wore baggy green camouflage pants and black army boots that he'd use on your face if you happened to look at him the wrong way. He always smelled like a combination of cigarettes and motor oil. His head was shaved in a crew cut.

"I wish somebody would kill that guy," Brodie whis-

13

pered, shaking his head. Then something caught his attention and he straightened up. "There he is."

"Who?" I'd forgotten why we were standing there in the first place.

"Mountain."

"Where?"

"Right there. You're looking at him."

"That's him?"

"That's him."

I felt a smile come to my face. "Wait a minute," I said. "I want to make sure we're talking about the same guy." I pointed. "Him?"

"That's the one," Brodie said.

This guy was short and stocky, with curly red hair and nerdy brown slacks that were too tight for his thick legs.

"You say he's a running back. With a good stiff-arm."

"Yep," Brodie said.

Well, I felt a wave of relief. This guy just didn't look like the type who could ruin my football season.

He stopped to watch Playchek and the ninth-grader.

The kid had fallen on the floor and Playchek was standing over him with his hands on his hips, telling him to get up. When he wouldn't, Playchek bent over and picked him up by the shirt collar.

Then Mountain did a strange thing. He walked right up to Playchek and tapped him on the shoulder.

Brodie grabbed my arm. "What's he doing? Oh, man, he doesn't know what he's doing—Hey, Mountain!"

Brodie hurried over to him. I followed.

"Hey, Mountain!"

Playchek had let the ninth-grader slump back to the floor. A few people stopped to watch.

"Can I help you?" Playchek said to Mountain. It was a funny thing for him to say in that grunt-squeal voice of his. A couple of people laughed nervously.

Brodie took Mountain by the arm and started to pull him away. "Come on, Paul," he said. "You don't want to get mixed up in this."

I had to give Brodie credit. Not many people would have had the guts to do something like that. Definitely not me.

Mountain looked at Brodie as if he wasn't speaking English. The guy didn't understand that Brodie was trying to save his life. He jerked his arm away from Brodie and turned back to Playchek.

"Why don't you leave the kid alone," Mountain said.

Playchek pointed at the kid he'd just dropped on the floor.

"Him?"

"Yeah. He's had enough."

"What business is it of yours?" Playchek said.

Brodie grabbed Mountain's arm again and pulled harder. "He's new. I'll get him out of here."

I tell you, I had to admire Brodie's bravery.

"Let him alone, dickface," Playchek said. Brodie let go of Mountain and backed up. His bravery had peaked.

Playchek turned back to Mountain. "You a freshman?"

"No. Sophomore."

"New in town?"

Mountain nodded.

"What's your name?"

"Paul Mountain."

"My name's Byron. Byron Playchek. Nice to meet you." Playchek stuck out his hand.

15

Mountain looked at Playchek's big stump of a hand. I think it was dawning on him that he wasn't talking to a reasonable human being. He reached out cautiously and shook hands.

"Know what I was beating this kid up for?" Playchek asked, grinning.

"No..." Mountain tried to smile, but it looked stiff.

"I just don't happen to like people with zits on their face," Playchek said.

Mountain chuckled uneasily.

"Something funny?" Playchek said, losing his smile.

"Well—"

And just like that, Playchek slugged him in the stomach. Mountain's eyes bulged and the wind whooshed out of him as he doubled over. Then Playchek clubbed him on top of his head, and Mountain sprawled to his hands and knees, holding the back of his neck.

"I think I'm getting sick," Brodie muttered.

So was I. The five-minute bell rang.

"Now you just stay there, dude," Playchek said, pointing a fat finger at Mountain. "You stay put till I'm gone. You know who I am now, right?"

Mountain didn't look up.

"Hey. I'm talking to you, zitface. You hear what I said?"

Still on his hands and knees, Mountain lifted his head. His whole body was shaking. "Yeah. I heard," he said.

Then he charged. Just like a lineman coming out of a four-point stance, Mountain yelled and charged and rammed his head into Playchek's belly and they both slammed into the opposite side of the locker bay. I could see the astonished look on Playchek's face as his back hit those lockers. Mountain straightened up and started swinging. He landed two quick left jabs that snapped Playchek's head back, then a hard right that landed against Playchek's nose and made a loud crack. Playchek's eyes fluttered and went glassy, and with his back still against the lockers, he slithered to the floor.

That's when the teachers showed up.

By the end of the day the whole school knew that Byron Playchek had gotten his face pounded by some new sophomore. Both Mountain and Playchek were suspended for the rest of the week.

Nobody knew anything about Paul Mountain except what Brodie and a couple of other guys had found out when they'd talked to him at the touch-football game. When people heard he was turning out for the football team they all said things like, "Wow, if he can do that to Playchek, he'll be a star in football!"

That didn't make me feel too good. I'll have to admit I was kind of glad to hear that Mountain had been suspended. That meant he wouldn't be able to show up for football until Monday. He'd be missing the first critical week of practices, where we'd be learning plays, audibles, formations, and all that. There were only nine practices until 66 Day—*the* big day. It was the day you found out whether or not you made varsity.

There's a story behind why it's called 66 Day. Our

school colors are gold and green: if you're on varsity, you wear a gold helmet; if you're on either JV or the freshman team, you wear a green helmet. About fifty years ago, 66 Day was called "Gold and Green Day." Over the years it got shortened to "G and G Day," then "GG Day." Then, about twenty years ago, there was this guy named Donny Schultz, who was a star offensive guard, with scholarship offers from all over the country. But instead of going to college he joined the army and went to Vietnam and wound up getting killed. It was the biggest thing to happen to this town for years. Well, Donny Schultz's jersey number happened to be 66. Now his jersey's on display in the trophy case in the Intersection, next to all of Clover Park's State Championship trophies, and that's how GG Day turned into 66 Day.

So you see, 66 Day isn't just a day when the coaches tack up a sheet of paper with a list of names on it. No, at Clover Park, it's a real event, a tradition. It always comes on the Friday of the second full week of football practices, and there's a school-wide assembly and Coach Wills stands on the gym floor in front of this rack full of gold helmets and one by one calls the name of every guy who made varsity. Each guy comes down, takes a helmet, and stands in line. Everybody cheers for the forty guys standing down there holding their gold helmets. Then school lets out early, football practice is canceled for the day, and one of the seniors has an all-night varsity-only kegger, and let me tell you, if you happen to be one of the three or four sophomores who are lucky enough to get a gold helmet on 66 Day, you become a Somebody real fast. Even if you've been a Nobody from grade nine on down to kindergarten.

I knew how important those next eight practices were going to be. I felt nervous as I suited up that afternoon. I've been suiting up for football practice every fall since Pee Wee's in fifth grade. I always do it in the same order: first my jock; then shoulder pads; practice jersey over the shoulder pads; socks; the lumpy pants stuffed with hip, knee, and thigh pads; then I tuck in the jersey, pull the belt tight, and put on my shoes.

I slammed my locker shut and went to the drinking fountain to rinse off my mouth guard. All over the JV locker room guys were slamming their lockers shut. I could hear the words "Mountain" and "Playchek" and "blood" and "running back" and "suspended" and "66 Day" coming from different places.

I headed up to the practice field by myself. I kept my head down and concentrated on my black Nike football shoes. My stomach got tighter and tighter as I walked up that grassy hill. My jock was digging into the inside of my thighs. It wouldn't be September without jock itch.

I was carrying my helmet by the face mask, and with each step I thumped it against my thigh pad. Thump, thump, thump. I could feel the sun starting to cook the back of my neck. As I walked, I was thinking that if I made varsity I wouldn't mind getting the crap knocked out of me by guys like Kortum. Those same guys would chat with me in the Intersection between classes. That new girl with the suntan who'd said Hi to me today would pass through the Intersection on her way to class and say to herself, "Wow, that Roger, he's only a sophomore, but he sure must be a Somebody to hang around with those guys. He probably wouldn't even want to waste his time with an unknown girl like me." Then one day, out of the blue, her phone would ring and she'd hear, "Hi, this is

21

Roger Ottosen. You want to go out this Friday?" and she'd be so stunned she'd barely even be able to say yes.

By now I'd made it to the top of the hill. I was crossing the jogging track when I heard the scratchy footsteps of a runner on the track coming toward me.

I looked up. I could hardly see because of the sun, so I squinted my eyes. For a second I thought I was seeing an illusion of what I'd just been thinking. But it wasn't any illusion, it was the real person, that new girl with the suntan. She was wearing white shorts and a blue Seahawks T-shirt.

"Hi there, Roger," she said, smiling and slowing to a walk. She was out of breath and her cheeks were red. She walked a few steps past me on the track, then stopped. Her legs were long and tanned.

"Hi," I said. Only it sounded more like "*Hg.*" I felt my throat close up and my face tighten. I couldn't say anything else.

We stood about six feet apart. I tried not to stare at her long legs.

"I thought I'd run the course," she said.

"It goes through the woods," I said.

"Yeah."

She stood there nodding, with her hands on her hips. Maybe she was a little uncomfortable, too. But all I could think of was, "I am ugly and stupid; I am ugly and stupid and a Nobody. Why would she want to talk to me anyway?"

"Hey, Ottosen, you bum!"

A couple of guys in football uniforms jogged past on the way to the practice field. Who they were didn't even register in my brain, but they gave me an excuse to look at something, so I kept my eyes on them for a long time.

"Well..." she said. "See you around."

She gave me a little wave and started off. My brain told me to say something to her—anything.

"Thanksalot!"

I don't know if she heard it or not, because she had already turned around and started jogging, but I'm pretty sure it's about the stupidest thing I've ever said. My brain just malfunctioned, like having mud come out of a drinking fountain instead of water.

Somebody shoved me from behind. It was Brodie. He was wearing his helmet and had his mouth protector in his mouth. "Well, who is she?" he asked.

I watched her jog along the track and turn off onto the trail into the woods.

"I don't know."

He stared at me and spat out his mouth protector. It was connected to his face mask, so it just kind of bobbed up and down between us.

"Didn't you ask her?"

"Ask her what?"

"Her name, you hamburger."

"I forgot."

"You forgot."

"My mind just went blank. I—I can't talk to girls. I give up. I'm hopeless."

There wasn't much he could say to that, except agree, so we just headed across the grass to the south goalposts and the first official practice of the season.

WE FORMED a circle for calisthenics, with Kortum and Hiddleston in the center, leading the count. As we did our sit-ups, the assistant coaches—all five of them—weaved in and out of the circle, yelling and clapping their hands to get us pumped up. They were all wearing gold caps with the initials CP on them and windbreakers that read "Logger Football." Coach Wills, our head coach, just stood and watched. He had a ton of class. That's what everybody said about him, that he had class and was a genius.

Calisthenics were always the easiest part of practice. After that, things got a lot rougher.

Like wind sprints. Coach Taller, the backfield coach, stood at the starting line. As each group of four came to the line he would yell, "Set!" and we'd get down into a three-point stance, then "Hut!" and we'd sprint forty yards to the finish line, jog back, line up, and do it again.

As far as I knew, there were only two or three guys on the team faster than me—Dalquist, a senior wide receiver; Zollenbeck, a junior who played safety and returned punts; and maybe Hiddleston. Hogness, the senior who'd probably start at running back, was pretty slow, so I made sure I got into his group of four. I knew this was my chance to stand out.

I beat Hogness by a good six feet. As we turned around to jog back to the other end, I glanced at Coach Wills, but he was watching the next group of runners.

I won every sprint. By the third set of ten, only a few of us could do more than trot for the forty yards. Zollenbeck got yelled at for not getting back into line right away. Kortum was wheezing like an accordion.

But I just kept thinking, 66 Day... 66 Day... 66 Day. I never caught Coach Wills looking right at me, but when I was finishing ten yards ahead of everybody else, I knew he was watching me. He had to be.

Next came the one-on-one tackling drill. It was the drill I hated most. The quarterback handed off to the running back, who had about five yards to put a move on the tackler. Most of the backs just gave a little fake and then plowed head-on into the tackler. But I didn't have the size to plow into those big seniors. I had to use every move I knew.

My first time up was against one of our best linebackers, Steve Reedy. I got the ball, faked left, then darted right. He got an arm around my waist, but I spun out of it and ran free. Some of the guys clapped.

"Come on, Reedy!" Coach Taller growled. "Get out there and do it again."

Reedy flattened the next guy.

"That's more like it," Taller said. I smiled to myself.

Next I had Zollenbeck, who was pretty quick. As I

took the handoff and angled right, he dove for my legs. I cut left, broke his tackle, and sprinted free and clear.

Taller just shook his head and scowled; Coach Wills was looking down at his clipboard. But my freshman coach from last year, Mr. Hill, clapped his hands and said, "Good job, Roger!"

Then I went against Kortum.

He waited in his four-point stance like a bull ready to charge. He'd hit the last ball carrier so hard the guy's helmet flew off.

I had about two seconds to decide what I was going to do before I was handed the ball. I started praying, "Don't let me fumble. God, please, don't let me fumble."

I took the handoff and ran as hard as I could right at him. Just as he was about to hit me, I buried the ball in my stomach, lowered my helmet, and twisted my body to the right so he wouldn't get a straight shot. He nailed me, but I held on to the ball, and actually fell forward a couple of yards.

"Two yard gain, right there, Kortum," Taller said, half smiling.

"Yeah, yeah," Kortum muttered, shaking his head and helping me up.

And right then I knew I was going to make varsity. I knew it because Kortum helped me up, and because for the first time I saw that Coach Wills was looking straight at me.

As I trotted to the end of the line, a few guys clapped their hands and slapped me on the helmet, because they knew it, too. Brodie, over in the tacklers' line, held up his fist and shook it at me. He knew. I was gasping like mad, not because I was tired but because I felt like I was going to burst out crying. I said over and over, "Thank you, God. Thank you. You're not going to regret this. I swear you're not."

After practice the JV locker room was dead quiet. We knew we were going to be worked this hard for eight more practices until 66 Day. It was so quiet I heard the door of the locker room swing open and the footsteps coming.

Coach Taller stopped in my row as I was pulling off my shoulder pads.

"Ottosen."

I looked up. "Right here."

"Stop by my office when you finish dressing."

His footsteps echoed away, the locker room door swung shut again, and then everybody started razzing me and throwing their used bloody tape at me and telling me how I'd better pack up right now and move my stuff to the varsity locker room. Brodie shoved me around a little, which made me realize how many bruises I had. But I didn't care.

I took my time showering and getting dressed before going into the varsity locker room to Taller's office. The JV locker room always smelled like Ben-Gay, while the varsity locker room smelled like Right Guard, English Leather, and Johnson's baby powder. That's just one of the differences between varsity and JV.

I knocked on Taller's door and heard, "Come in."

Taller turned around in his chair and faced me.

Then I saw who was sitting on one corner of his desk. It was Coach Wills. He was looking at a sheet of paper in his hand.

I hadn't expected him to be in this office; he had his

own office farther down the corridor. He didn't look at me. He was studying that piece of paper. All of a sudden I was terrified.

Finally Taller took off his glasses and said, "You worked your tail off out there today, Roger. I just want to tell you to keep it up. We're weak at running back this year. We might have to take a sophomore from JV, even though we don't usually like to do that. But we might have to." He put his glasses back on. "Now, get a good night's sleep tonight."

"Okay," I said.

Coach Wills looked up from the piece of paper in his hand. "You got a D in math last year. No D's this year, son."

I just stared at him for a second, like an idiot. That's when I figured out what he was holding. It was a copy of my final report card from last year.

All I could do was nod as Coach Taller held the door open for me.

5

WELL, I may not be the brightest guy in Clover Park, but I could sure figure out what it meant when the head coach himself took the time to tell you to do your homework and not get any D's. It meant, "Don't go screwing around in your classes, because you have to keep a decent grade point average in order to be on varsity."

I went outside and took a deep breath. Fall was in the air. Football. I could feel it all around me. Somehow I felt like everything was right in the world. This was my year.

I forgot all my bruises and sore muscles from practice and started running down the sidewalk, carrying my notebook like a football, putting a move every few yards on a telephone pole or a stop sign or a dog, leaping driveways, cutting across people's lawns, a stadium full of fans cheering me on. I started up the hill to my house and went right by it, past the vacant wooded lots at the end of the street, to the foot of the bluff. I took one long look, put my head down, and charged. Halfway up, I felt like I was going to die. But I dug in and made it to the top.

When I started to regain my breath, I looked out across the valley of trees and houses and, beyond it, the town. I felt like a different person up there on the bluff, like I could do anything, like there weren't all kinds of things always pushing at me and trying to get in my way. Why couldn't I feel like this all the time?

I walked back down the bluff to my house, but nobody was there. That meant Mom probably wouldn't be home till eight or nine. Mom's housekeeper, Mrs. Wynn, had fixed some chili for my dinner, so all I had to do was toss it in the microwave for a couple of minutes, flip on the TV, and start eating.

We have a housekeeper because Mom works about fourteen hours a day, seven days a week. She's a realtor, and a very good one at that. Last year she got Honorable Mention for the Clover Park Realtor-of-the-Year Award. And she's only thirty-five years old. This year she wants to win that award.

She married my stepdad, Art, right when I finished eighth grade. It was all kind of sudden. I knew Mom and Art had been friends for a few years, but one day Mom asked me what I thought about Art. I said I thought he was okay. Then she asked me what I thought about her marrying the guy.

"*Art?* Why would you want to marry Art?" I had asked.

She laughed and said she loved him. "Not the same way I loved your dad," she said, "but this is a little more secure and stable kind of love. I know Art's getting on in years and he's got a rough surface, but once you get to know the real Art, I promise you'll like him."

They got married in June and went to Ireland for their honeymoon, while I stayed at Brodie's. When they came back, we moved to this big new house up on the hill, where all these doctors and lawyers live. I had a tough time saying goodbye to the old neighborhood where Brodie and I had grown up two houses apart.

I'm not really sure how old Art is. Brodie's mom says he's "pushing sixty," and Brodie's mom usually knows that kind of stuff. Art's still got his hair and everything, and it's not even entirely gray, but he slicks it straight back in that old-man style. Brodie's mom says Art has more money than even Mom or I know about. He's lived in Clover Park all his life, and made his money owning land and building residential neighborhoods, like the one we live in. He was married once before Mom; he even has a couple of grown-up sons from his first marriage. The sons and the ex-wife all live in California, and the sons won't even speak to him.

Some people probably think Mom married Art for his money. But I know she didn't. She really loves him, I can tell. She kids him a lot and calls him the Old Man, but I've seen the way she looks at him sometimes, and the way she laughs at him when he's being grouchy, and I know she'd love him no matter what.

I was eating my second bowl of chili and watching *The Three Stooges* when Art came home from the club. Now that he's "semi-retired," he plays a round of golf every day at the Clover Park Golf and Tennis Club, then poker afterward in the men's locker room.

"How's business there, pardner," he said in his gruff voice as he came into the family room. He used to smoke two packs a day, and his voice still sounded like it. Mom made him quit smoking—although sometimes when she's not home I walk by his office upstairs and smell cigarette smoke coming from under the door.

33

"Pretty good," I said.

He went over to the bar in the corner of the family room and started fixing himself a drink. That's the first thing he does when he gets home from the club.

He squinted at the TV. I could hear his loud breathing. We both looked at a commercial for "Twenty-five Love Songs of the Eighties," $9.95 for record, $11.95 for tape. The ice tinkled in his glass as he took a sip.

"Connie home yet?" he asked, still squinting at the TV.

"No, I just got home from practice."

"Football practice, eh?"

"Yep."

He nodded and took another sip. I finished off the chili and went out to the kitchen and dished up some peanut-butter/chocolate-chip ice cream.

Art was still standing in the middle of the family room.

"Newspaper come?" he asked.

"Yeah, it's on the hall chair. I'll get it."

"No, no, I'll get it."

Most evenings he'd sit in his easy chair with a drink and read the Clover Park *Chronicle,* front to back. Sometimes he'd peer over the top of the paper at whatever TV show I was watching. He and I just never seemed to have much to say to each other. In spite of what Mom said before she married him, about me getting underneath his rough surface, I really didn't know him, and he sure didn't know me. Art's a tough guy to get comfortable with. I always wonder what he must've been like around his own sons. He's always saying how he "flunked fatherhood." He says it jokingly, but it's got to be a little weird

34

having a couple of sons who won't even send you a lousy Christmas card.

It was eight-thirty when Mom got home. She put her briefcase on the kitchen table, slipped off her shoes, and came into the family room in her stocking feet.

Suddenly the whole room seemed to brighten. Art lowered his newspaper.

"Well, well, well," he said. "Get you a drink?"

"Oh, please. Hi there!" she said to me, smiling and still a little out of breath. "Mrs. Wynn leave dinner for you?" She asked me that almost every night.

"Yep."

Then she just kind of fell down on the couch in a heap. You could tell she'd been moving all day long, and this one motion of falling onto the couch meant that she was done moving for the day. Sometimes she'd come home and not fall onto the couch, which meant she had business going on that evening, or she and Art had some party to go to or something. I always liked it when she fell onto the couch in a heap.

I turned off the TV, because I knew she hated it, and turned on the stereo to the Lite-Rock station. She sat there with her head resting against the back of the couch, taking little sips of her drink.

After a while she turned to me. "Well, how was the first day of school?"

"Okay," I said, wishing I was still in that cocky mood I'd been in on the bluff.

"How are your classes?"

"Not bad."

She smiled. "Lots of cute girls?"

Art peered at me from over his newspaper.

"I guess," I shrugged.

"Meet any new people?" she asked.

I thought of that new girl with the tan. "Nah."

"Well," Mom said, tapping her mouth with her finger, "tell me the best thing that happened to you all day."

I thought of the girl with the tan again, but put her out of my mind. "Football practice," I said.

"Oh! How was it? Tell me how it was."

I started nodding. Mom knew how important these first two weeks of practice were. "It was...it was pretty good," I said.

"Yeah?"

"They called me into their office. They said I looked good."

Mom leaned forward. "Wait a minute, now. Who called you into their office? Taller?"

"Yeah. And—and Wills was in there, too."

"Wills! What did he say?"

"He told me I did a good job."

"Are you the only one they called in?"

"Yeah. They—they kind of hinted I'd make varsity."

Her mouth fell open and she slapped her leg. "I knew it! Art, didn't I tell you he had a chance at varsity this year? Now, when's 66 Day? A week from this Friday, isn't it?"

"Yeah," I said.

She smiled. It made me feel good to see her looking so proud.

"I just knew you could do it," she said. "All the work you put into it this summer. All the running and work-outs. Varsity as a sophomore! Oh, Roger!"

She leaned over and gave me a hug. I reached down and fiddled with the balance knob on the stereo.

"Varsity halfback and number one on the tennis team," she said to Art. "How do you like those credentials?"

"Pretty darn good," Art said.

"How did the Mountain boy look?" Mom asked after a while.

I looked at her and blinked. "What?"

"Mountain. Didn't you see him?"

"How'd you know about him?"

"Didn't I tell you?"

"Tell me what?"

"I'm sure I told you the other day. I sold the Mercer house to Marc Mountain—his father."

Art looked up from his newspaper. "What did you say?"

"You mean I didn't tell you, either?"

"No, you didn't tell me," he said.

"The Mercer house. The one with the tennis court."

"I know the Mercer house," he said. "Come to think of it, you might've told me at that." He went back to his newspaper.

"You didn't tell me," I said. You could see the Mercer house from the top of the bluff, although you couldn't see the tennis court because it was hidden by trees. Suddenly the thought of a tennis court gave me a sick feeling. I looked at Mom. "He plays tennis, too?"

"Who?"

"Mountain."

She shrugged. "Hm. I'm not sure." She looked at Art. "Marc Mountain owns Tallchief Resort."

"I've heard of it," Art said.

37

So had I. It was a tennis resort and ranch in eastern Washington, where all these rich people went to ride horses and play tennis. They sent their stuck-up kids there, too.

"Why would Marc Mountain move to Clover Park?" I asked.

"His wife. She's the new women's athletic director at the college." Mom thought for a minute. "Actually, no, I don't think the boy plays tennis. Maybe just football. He has a twin sister, too. Mary Jo or Mary Jane or something. How did he look?"

"Who, Mountain? I don't know, he wasn't there."

"I thought he was turning out. Why wasn't he there?"

I told her about the fight.

"That doesn't sound like him at all," Mom said. "When I met him, he seemed awfully meek and shy." She turned to Art. "You know, Art, they've joined the club."

Art was dozing in the chair.

"Art. They've joined the club."

He woke up.

"Huh? Who's joined the club?"

Mom just looked at me and shook her head and smiled.

6

THAT FIRST WEEK of school was amazing. I paid attention in class because I knew the coaches might be checking up on me with my teachers. Practices went great. Oh, I still felt butterflies while I suited up in the locker room, but at least I could eat lunch without feeling sick. I even seemed more popular—but maybe that was my imagination. Maybe I was just seeing everything reflected in a gold football helmet.

On Friday of that first wonderful week, Brodie and I happened to be standing in the Intersection when that new girl came walking by again. She smiled at me. I was kind of slouching against the wall, and when I saw her I tensed up. I wanted to go up to her and say something, but I was too chicken.

"Go on, you idiot!" Brodie gave me a shove. "Go talk to her!"

I held my breath and took off after her.

"How do you like Clover Park?" I asked, catching up

with her. I knew Brodie was watching me, so I couldn't run away.

"It's all right," she said.

Then my mind went blank. Fortunately, though, she said what I was trying to remember to ask.

"My name's Mary Jo Mountain. I thought I might as well tell you."

"You're Paul's twin sister?" I said. "You don't look like him."

She shrugged. We walked down the hall together.

"I saw you at the tennis club one day," she said, looking at me. "The first week we moved here. You were teaching a class of little kids outside."

"Oh, really?"

"Of course I had no idea who you were then, but I went into that lounge area where they have the bulletin board, and there was this newspaper clipping that had a picture of you swinging a tennis racquet. It said something like, 'City Champ for 16-and-Unders,' and it had your name. So you stuck in my mind. You must be pretty good. See you later."

She turned off down another hallway. I just stood there watching her. I began to feel that old feeling creep over me. I'd gotten it every year since sixth grade. It was that horrible, awful sensation of starting to have a crush on a girl. All kinds of weird feelings are mixed up in it, but you can't really identify any of them. It's hell.

On Monday, her brother came back to school.

As I was suiting up for practice, I said to myself: Only four practices till 66 Day. What can he possibly do in four practices?

When it came time for wind sprints, I got down into

my three-point stance with Paul Mountain right beside me. I'd planned it that way.

"Set... Hut!"

I gave that forty yards everything I had. I saw Mountain out of the corner of my eye. We started out even, then I pulled away from him and ended up beating him by five yards.

I beat him every time. He wasn't used to these wind sprints, and by the second set of ten he was puffing and trotting along with everybody else, while I kept sprinting.

Then it was time for the one-on-one tackling drill. The first time Mountain got the ball, he looked confused, like he didn't know quite what to do. He stood up straight and Brodie nailed him in the stomach and drove him back five yards.

"Get down lower there," one of the coaches said. "What's your name?"

"Mountain."

"Well, get down lower there, Morton."

Taller just spat; Wills was busy looking at his clipboard. I couldn't help smiling.

I went up against Drew Rover, a sophomore. He dove for the fake I gave him and I glided right past him.

The next time Mountain got the ball, he seemed to understand what to do with it. He was up against Dave Tordzik, a varsity guard. Tordzik came at him in a crouch, with his arms out. Mountain held the ball against his belly with both hands, lowered his helmet, and ran straight ahead. There was a loud crack of helmets. Mountain ran over him. Tordzik didn't get up. A couple of coaches and managers finally got Tordzik to his feet and took him to the locker' room for an early shower.

Then Mountain went against Tony Varnes, a tall,

skinny senior. Varnes let out a roar as he came for Mountain, who tucked the ball in his left arm and angled to the left. Just as Varnes was going to hit him, Mountain stiff-armed him in the face with his right arm and broke the tackle.

Coach Wills lowered his clipboard.

Coach Taller asked, "What was your name again, there?"

"Mountain."

Brodie came over to me from the tacklers' line and whispered, "I told you he had a mean stiff-arm."

I didn't say anything.

On his next turn, Mountain came up against Kortum. I wanted Kortum to crunch him. Maybe even do a little more than that.

Mountain took the handoff and ran straight ahead. He didn't veer to the left and he didn't veer to the right. He just ran straight ahead.

It was a head-on collision.

When they collided, there was an explosion. Both of them seemed to freeze for a second. They just stood there. Then Kortum dropped to his knees. Mountain staggered a couple of steps, regained his senses, and trotted past Kortum for a touchdown.

Coach Taller and Coach Wills looked at each other.

Practice continued. Mountain carried the ball a couple more times, but nobody seemed too eager to tackle him.

After practice, Taller called Mountain into his office and talked to him for a long time.

Brodie turned to me while we were getting dressed and shook his head. "It looks like you two are in a real dogfight. You've still got the inside track. You're quicker and faster. And the coaches know you better. And, jeez, Mountain's only been turning out one lousy day. There's only three more practices till 66 Day. I don't see how they'd pick Mountain ahead of you. I seriously doubt it. But I don't know." He shook his head again. "I just don't know. It's a dogfight."

I listened closely to what he said because Brodie knew what he was talking about. He knew football, and he knew the coaches and the way their minds worked.

"You're two completely different kinds of running backs," he went on. "You're fast and wiry. He's a lunatic. It just depends on what kind of back they're looking for."

"Come on, Brodie, he's only been here one day."

Brodie nodded. "Yeah. That's why I'd have to bet on you. Hell, our first game is in ten days! He sure as heck doesn't seem bright enough to learn all the plays by then. He's not that bright, period, in case you haven't noticed. Nobody with any brains is gonna run head-on into Bob Kortum."

I nodded.

"Hell yeah," Brodie said, "my money's on you." But he kept shaking his head. "Jeesh!—you gotta admit, though, the guy's pretty amazing. Pretty damn amazing. I've never seen anything like him. Too bad he had to come along. You had it made. It's just tough luck."

Too bad . . . tough luck . . . I knew what all that meant. You're a Nobody, Ottosen.

43

7

WHEN 66 Day finally came, I hardly knew what I was doing. I just walked around in a daze. During lunch I didn't even attempt to look at food. Instead, I ended up at the library, sitting at a table and flipping through an old *Tennis Digest* magazine. I found it kind of comforting to look at pictures of tennis players. The night before, Mom had tried to act real optimistic, but I could see that she had on her salesperson smile. She knew what was happening. She knew Mountain and I had been in a dog-fight all week.

Out loud, she kept saying, "Well, you'll be number one in tennis. You have *that...*" And she would nod her head and smile. But her eyebrows kept wanting to go up into that look of pity I'd seen before, especially when she was saying something like, "Oh, you mean you're not taking a girl to the dance tonight?" Those were times when I would have given anything for her not to look at me that way. I just wanted her to be able to come to football games and cheer for me, as she used to do for my dad, and tell people, "That's my son. He's only a sophomore, can you believe it?"

Suddenly a hand came down on top of the picture I was looking at. The fingers were long and narrow, the fingernails short and painted pink. There was a ring on one of the fingers. It was a beautiful hand.

I looked up at Mary Jo Mountain.

She smiled. "Hi there."

She was leaning on my table, looking down at me. This was the closest I'd ever been to her. I could see the freckles on the bridge of her nose and smell the grape gum she was chewing. An uncontrollable blush washed over me and I knew she could see how red my face was. Why did she even bother to try to talk to me at all? I leaned back in my seat and tried not to look as awkward as I felt.

"66 Day right after lunch, right?" she said, chewing her gum.

"Don't remind me," I said.

"God, it's such a big deal around here. It's all any-body's talking about."

"Yeah."

"My brother was all nervous this morning. He couldn't eat any breakfast." She shook her head. "Usually he eats a huge breakfast."

She had both of her hands on the table. Her arms were right there next to my face. Brown skinny arms with little blond hairs. And a silver bracelet that was kind of sexy.

"I'm a little nervous about it, too," I said. It wasn't a bad thing to say.

"My brother talked about you."

"He did?"

"He said you're fast."

"Really?"

"Yeah." Then she said, "He doesn't think he can beat you."

"You mean in a race?"

"Well, that too. I mean in varsity."

"He doesn't?"

"No."

"He doesn't know that," I said. "Nobody does." I looked down at a picture of John McEnroe in the magazine. "You guys have a tennis court," I said. "Does Paul play tennis?"

"Paul is too uncoordinated. You wouldn't believe how klutzy he is at things like tennis. He's only good at sports that he can be a maniac in. Like football and skiing. Skiing is his favorite. That's the only time he kind of perks up, when he's skiing. Everything else, he's clumsy."

"Who uses the tennis court, then?"

"My dad and me. But I like playing at the club better. I thought I'd go there today after school. To use the ball machine."

"That's good practice," I said.

"Sometimes I wear my Walkman."

"While you're using the ball machine?"

"Yeah."

"I never thought of that," I said. "I suppose it would be pretty good when you're just standing there hitting ground strokes."

"You're on the tennis team, aren't you? Everybody says you'll be number one."

"Well, you never know for sure," I said. "Are you turning out for the girls' team this fall?"

She made a face and shrugged. "I thought about it.

47

But I didn't want to. I don't see why the girls should have to play in the fall. It rains too much."

"It rains a lot in the spring, too. We get rained out all the time."

"My old school had three indoor courts."

"Really? Where was that?"

She told me, and that started her talking about her old school, and about how she missed her best friend, while I just sat there watching her lips and looking at her teeth. Her tongue was purple from the grape gum. I forgot about 66 Day.

But then she had to go and remind me. "Do you have football practice this afternoon?" she asked.

"No. We get the day off because it's 66 Day."

"Well," she said, straightening up and looking around, "I'll be at the club after the assembly. Maybe I'll run into you there."

"Yeah," I said. "Uh...your brother really doesn't think he'll make varsity?"

"The coaches called him up a couple of nights ago."

"What?"

"They called him up and talked to him for a long time. I don't know what they talked to him about, but after he hung up he told Mom he didn't think he was going to make varsity because he'd only been to four practices."

"I wonder what they told him," I said. "I wonder why they called him."

"I don't know," she said, "but I don't think he minds being on JV. See you this afternoon, maybe."

She turned and walked away. I was going to say something to her, tell her, "I'll be there!" or offer to walk to the assembly with her or something. But just as I stood up, she opened the library door and disappeared into the crowd of people heading to the assembly.

I was smiling. She liked me enough to carry on a conversation with me, and her brother had practically been told by the coaches that he wouldn't make varsity. It was like this huge weight had been lifted off me, and I just stood there in the library, feeling as if I was floating up to the ceiling, with a dumb grin on my face.

Suddenly I had to yell. I had this yell inside of me that wanted to escape. It almost came out right there in the library, but I managed to hurry to my locker. The hallway was crowded with people on their way to the gym, but pretty soon it cleared. I opened my locker, stuck my head inside, buried my face in my letterman's jacket, and let out a scream that lasted for about ten seconds. But it didn't stop there; it turned into a kind of hysterical high-pitched laughter.

A lone ninth-grade girl happened to be walking by. She hurried past, looked back at me over her shoulder, and hurried faster.

I let her get around the corner before I grabbed my letterman's jacket and headed off to the assembly.

8

IN THE GYM, the ninth- and tenth-graders sat in the visitors' bleachers, and the eleventh- and twelfth-graders were in the home bleachers opposite them. At one end of the gym floor, the pep band sat in folding chairs and played the Clover Park fight song, while late students straggled in and looked for places to sit. I spotted Brodie about ten rows up, waving at me, so I climbed my way to him.

Back down on the floor, the eight cheerleaders, elected last spring, were going through their routine. Whenever I see them I always think of how my mom must have jumped around on that gym floor eighteen 66 Days ago, while my dad was up here in these bleachers, waiting for his name to be called.

The Rally Girls, too young to be real cheerleaders this year, were wearing gold-and-green dresses and standing up and shaking their little gold-and-green pom-poms to the fight song. Mr. Hopkins, the vice principal, was standing at the microphone, waiting for everybody to get settled.

Down in the middle of the floor was the rack of forty gold helmets. Coach Wills and the assistant coaches were sitting in folding chairs next to them.

Mr. Hopkins signaled for the band to stop playing. The cheerleaders walked over to the side and sat down on the floor with their legs tucked under them.

Mr. Hopkins cleared his throat into the microphone. "Let's all rise for the National Anthem."

The whole time this was going on, I was trying to tell myself that I was going to make it. I kept going over that conversation with Mary Jo, but now it seemed like it hadn't even happened. I kept praying over and over again, "God, please let this happen for me."

As we sat down after the Pledge of Allegiance, Brodie looked at me and said in a voice that didn't sound like him at all, "Damn, Roger, I'm nervous." He looked as if he was going to throw up.

Mr. Hopkins began his annual 66 Day speech. He talked about Donny Schultz, the guy who had been killed in Vietnam; he talked about school spirit, sportsmanship, how our football team always dominated the league, and how we always helped our opponents up after we knocked the you-know-what out of 'em. That got a big laugh. Mr. Hopkins grinned, pushed his glasses up to his face, and waited for the laughter to stop.

Then he went into a long introduction of Coach Wills. For the next few minutes, as Coach Wills went up to the microphone, there was nothing but cheering. He stood at the mike, waiting for everybody to be quiet, and a couple of times he said, "Let's get this started," but the cheering kept on. Finally Mr. Hopkins ran out onto the floor holding his hands up, and about a minute after that everybody sat down.

After introducing his coaching staff, Coach Wills said: "Now I'm going to read off the names of this year's varsity football squad."

The gym got very quiet.

"The first young man I'm going to introduce really needs no introduction at all. Everybody knows he's the guts and backbone of this football team. A straight-A student, All-Conference and All-State last year as a junior defensive linebacker, Mr. Bob Kortum."

The crowd went crazy.

Kortum walked down to the floor, wearing jeans and a white T-shirt that showed off about twelve different sets of muscles. He towered over most of the coaches as he shook their hands. The senior section started up a chant, "*Kor-tum...Kor-tum...Kor-tum*," and then the freshmen, sophomores, and juniors joined in. It was an awesome sound. Kortum just stood there, not smiling, holding his gold helmet at his side.

Finally it quieted down, and Coach Wills was able to introduce the other captain, the quarterback of the Clover Park Loggers, All-Conference and Second-String All-State, Julian Hiddleston.

Everybody went wild again. The ninth-grade girls screamed like he was some rock star walking across the gym floor. Hiddleston shook hands with all the coaches and took a gold helmet off the rack. He and Kortum grinned at each other as they shook hands. They were probably thinking about the party they were going to have that night. The two of them stood out there alone, side by side, the two gods, and everybody yelled for them.

After that, things went a little faster. Coach Wills an-

53

nounced all of the returning lettermen. One by one he called their names: first the eleven seniors, then the three juniors. Each of them walked down to the floor, took a helmet, and shook hands with Kortum and Hiddleston and all of the other guys standing in line. They didn't shake hands with the coaches. Only Kortum and Hiddleston had the privilege of doing that.

Next, Coach Wills announced the rest of the varsity, the ones who hadn't lettered last year. Most of them were juniors who had been sophomores on JV last year. Ordinary guys, if you know what I mean.

Coach Wills paused for a second, then said, "Folks, as you can see, there are still four gold helmets remaining on this rack. Those four helmets are going to a special group of individuals: sophomores."

I glanced over at Brodie and saw that he had his eyes closed. I held my breath.

Coach Wills continued: "It's not a small achievement to make the varsity football team in this school. But for a sophomore, it's nearly impossible. It takes an individual who has distinguished himself during every practice, in every single aspect of football. It takes somebody who's willing to study hard in school and get good grades. Needless to say, the four individuals I'm now going to call down have a very special honor, but they also have very special responsibilities. You tenth-graders can be proud of these representatives of your class."

That brought an outburst from the sophomore section, then it got quiet. Real quiet.

"The first person I want to call is Clay Brodie."

Brodie froze. His face went absolutely white. For a second I forgot about myself; I grabbed his hand and shook it hard.

54

He made his way down the bleachers to the floor and took the long walk to the helmet rack, while everybody cheered for him.

"The next person is Lee Edwards."

Nobody was too surprised to hear that Edwards had made it. He weighed almost two hundred pounds and could hold his own against the seniors.

"Next, Gordon Jeffers."

Jeffers had made it because he was a good place-kicker and punter. He played soccer in the spring.

One helmet left, one name to go. This was it. I realized I was biting my lower lip.

"This last person is a much needed running back who'll see a lot of action this year. I think we're going to get a few touchdowns from this young man...

"...Paul Mountain."

There it was. A bright light exploded in my head. For a second the flash blinded me.

All the nervousness went away. I sat and stared. Maybe I clapped.

When the assembly ended, I managed to avoid everybody and slip out through the locker-room exit. I didn't want to have to face Brodie or anybody else. I just started walking. I went up the grassy hill to the practice fields and along the jogging trail into the woods. I wandered through the woods, came out in an unfamiliar neighborhood, and walked past the houses without looking at them.

After a while, thoughts started flooding in, and they weren't pleasant. Right then, if there'd been a car coming toward me, I could have stepped in front of it. I really could have. My life wasn't worth a piece of dog crap. My hands inside my letterman's jacket were clenched in tight fists. I felt two things at the same time. Part of me wanted to get into a fight; the other part of me wanted to just lie down on the sidewalk and fold.

After about an hour, I realized my legs were taking me to the bluff. For the first time in almost four months, I walked up instead of running it. When I got to the top, I grabbed a handful of rocks and started throwing them as hard as I could at a tree that was about twenty yards away from me. My arm went sore— my tennis arm—but I didn't care. When I finished throwing all the rocks in my hand, I lay down on my back and looked up at the clouds. It was a sunny day, but you could feel the crispness in the air that meant fall, and football.

Right then I made up my mind to quit football forever. Just give it up. The hell with JV. What was the point of going through it all? The practices, the suiting up, the butterflies that came before games that didn't matter because they were JV games, played on Thursday afternoons in the mud. With nobody watching.

When I finally headed down the bluff, I felt a little better, now that I'd made up my mind. People would call me a quitter; the coaches would try to talk me out of it; Coach Wills would just look at me and not say anything. He'd be thinking, "I didn't know you were a quitter." Mom would be disappointed in me, too. It would be hell, but it would be over.

I got home and was relieved that nobody was there. I went upstairs to my room. In my desk, way in the back of the drawer, I kept a pack of Marlboros and a book of matches. I took a cigarette and lit it and stood looking out my bedroom window while I smoked. I took deep drags—it gave me a thrill to be doing something wicked. I smoked the cigarette right down to the butt. Then I lit up another. I used my wastebasket as an ashtray. So what if Mom found out?

I blew the smoke out my window and watched a wall of dark clouds roll in from the west. It was going to rain. Fall was here, summer was over. Halloween would be coming along in a month or so. All the big football games of October. The varsity players wearing their jerseys to school on game days...

Halfway through my fourth cigarette I remembered Mary Jo. She was at the club right now, maybe even waiting for me. I mean, she probably wasn't sitting around looking at her watch waiting for me, but at least in the back of her mind she was thinking, "I wonder if Roger's going to show up." Who knows, maybe she was even hoping Roger would show up. After all, she had asked me, sort of. It wasn't like I had invited myself or something.

I looked over at my tennis racquets leaning against the wall. My good old loyal tennis racquets.

Yeah, there was tennis this spring. Paul Mountain couldn't steal that away from me. Nobody could. Maybe I'd even be number one in the whole league. Mike Brock would be the only one who could stop me. But I knew I could beat Brock. I'd done it two weeks ago for the first time. While Brock was busy being a star at football and basketball for Hillside, I could be practicing tennis, gearing up for him in the league tournament this spring. And if I won the league tournament, I'd be invited to the state tournament in Spokane. A sophomore, making it to State.

Heck, if I worked hard enough, maybe I could *win* that state tournament.

I put my cigarette out in the wastebasket and changed into my sweats as fast as I could. I was pumped. I practically sprinted all the way to the club.

WHEN I got to the club, I went upstairs to the viewing
lounge to catch my breath. I was glad to see it was empty.
I rehearsed a few suave things to say to Mary Jo, like,
"Well, your brother certainly deserves congratulations."

Or, "Sorry I'm late. Say, maybe I could give you a few
pointers."

Or, "Sorry I'm late. Hey, what do you say I buy you a
Coke after we hit a few?"

I walked over to the windows that looked out on the
six indoor courts. Sure enough, there she was on court
number 4.

She was with somebody else.

Mike Brock.

My mouth fell open. I just stood there with my
mouth open, like a fish.

Somebody came into the lounge. It was Freddy Elliott, an obnoxious eighth-grader at my old junior high.
His dad was a dentist who told corny jokes and wore neck
scarves.

59

"Hey, I was sitting there, Roger. You're standing in front of my seat."

I was looking at Brock. He was at the net, talking to Mary Jo. They were both chatting and laughing. Brock was such a stud, and Mary Jo was standing there in that shy way girls do when they know they're talking to a stud. That summer I'd seen plenty of girls stand exactly the same way while they talked to Brock.

Elliott gave me a shove. "I saved that place with my racquet, Roger. It's right there, dude. I put my racquet right there to save that seat. It's mine."

"Shut up." I was still watching Brock.

"*You* shut up. That's my seat!"

I moved out of the way and let him have his stupid seat. He sat down and slurped an ice-cream bar.

"This is some match, Roger," he said.

"What?"

"Brock's getting beat by that chick."

"What are you talking about, bozo? They're not even playing. They're standing at the net talking."

"I know, *bozo*. They just finished the first set, *bozo*. That's why I went and got an ice cream, because they just finished their first set. And that chick won."

"How do you know?"

"Duh, take a guess! I was keeping track of the score. I've been up here for an hour. I was using the practice court and that chick took it after me. She started hitting on the ball machine. She was pretty good. Not to mention good-lookin'. I decided I'd come up here and watch her."

"Was she wearing a Walkman?" I asked.

"Huh?"

"Was she wearing a Walkman while she was using the ball machine?"

Elliott laughed. "What kind of a stupid question is that? No, she didn't have a Walkman. Pretty soon Brock comes up here and I give him change for a dollar and he buys a Coke. He stands right here, drinking his Coke, and we're both watching that chick hit ground strokes with the ball machine. Brock whistles and says, 'Will you look at that?'—or something like that. So he gives me his Coke and before I know it he's down there putting the hustle on that chick. I could tell. I can always tell when Brock's putting the hustle on some chick. Hee-hee! And she was goin' for it. Which ain't too surprising, considering all Brock has to do is snap his fingers."

I looked at them. They were still at the net, talking. What could they possibly be talking about?

Elliott went on. "Then they unplugged the ball machine and moved down to court 4 and started hitting. And next thing you know, they're both taking warm-up serves. Brock started out playing half-assed the first set, I think. He probably let her win the first few games."

"He probably let her win the whole set."

"Could be."

"What was the score?"

"Six—three. Yeah, could be he let her win. But she hit some killer shots. And, I'll tell you something, Roger. She had a 3—1 lead and Brock, he gets this look, like he says to himself, 'Okay, I've fooled around enough, I've got to show her who's boss.' But she still won the set. Brock's sweatin' up a storm. You can't tell me he ain't sweatin' up a storm."

They started another set, with Brock serving. He used his hard, flat cannonball. It was his hardest serve, all right, the same one he would've used against me. He wasn't holding anything back.

They rallied. Brock hit a good, deep approach shot and followed it to the net. Mary Jo ran to the ball, planted, cocked her two-fisted backhand, and belted the ball crosscourt. Brock barely got his racket on it and sent back a weak shot that bounced shallow. She ran up on it, bent down low, wound up, and blew it right past him.

"Wheeeeeyew!" Elliott screamed. "You see that, Roger? Hee-hee! That's what the whole first set was like. Brock's gettin' his clock cleaned! Hee-hee!"

I watched Mary Jo walk casually to her backhand court to receive the next serve. I looked at Brock for some reaction. I didn't see any, although he hit an extra-hard first serve, which Mary Jo returned with topspin. A rocket serve like that, most people would be lucky just to chip back a return, but she put everything she had into it. Then she just stayed on the baseline, real steady, moving Brock all around, working him out of position, then putting him away.

Elliott and I kept score. I watched every point carefully. I watched Mary Jo—her footwork, her rhythm, the way she cocked her racquet for those two-handed topspin backhands. Between points I watched her face. She was all business.

Brock stopped coming to the net after he realized she could pass him at will. But it was worse when he stayed back at the baseline; Mary Jo could place her ground strokes deep in either corner.

She won the set 6–4.

"They're gonna play another one," Elliott said, leaning forward and giggling. "Hee-hee! Oh, man, Brock wants revenge! Hee-hee-hee! Wait till everybody hears about this. Brock's getting goosed by a girl!"

That third set of theirs was close. It lasted a good forty minutes. A few other people gathered in the lounge to watch the match, and Elliott filled them in on what was happening. They all made comments like "Wow, she's really something!" although a lot of them couldn't believe Brock was really trying his hardest. That's what I wanted to think, too. But I knew one thing for sure: he was going to try his hardest *after* the match, when it was time to put the moves on her. And that made me feel kind of sick.

Mary Jo won the third set in a tiebreaker. Brock didn't look too happy as they walked over and sat down on the courtside bench. They stayed there and talked for a good ten minutes. Then they stood up and headed toward the lounge, probably to get a pop, so I got the heck out of there before they saw me.

I walked home in the darkness and rain.

Friday night. The varsity football team was celebrating somewhere with a keg. All around Clover Park, people were going out and doing things—dates, movies, bowling, cruising around, listening to music, making out. All this week I'd been filled with hope. Not only about making varsity. About everything. About girls. Like Mary Jo Mountain. Here was a beautiful girl, new in town, who was actually friendly toward me and knew my name. I thought I had a chance with her, maybe. But now I knew how stupid I was to have hoped for something like that. She'd been to 66 Day. And now she was with Brock. So much for that.

Mom and Art still weren't home. Then I remembered they'd gone to a dinner party and wouldn't be back till late. Mrs. Wynn had left me some pizza. I sat down in front of the TV with the remote control and flipped around to different channels.

The phone rang. I had a terrible feeling it was Mom and I didn't want to answer it. But I had to. If I didn't, she'd think I was out celebrating because I'd made varsity.

"Hello?"

"Hey, Rog!"

It wasn't Mom. It was Brodie.

"Roger! It shoulda been you, man!"

It was real noisy from where he was calling. I could hear voices and music in the background.

"You drunk?" I said.

"Hell no! Coupla kegs here. It shoulda been you here, man!"

He wouldn't have called me if he hadn't been drunk. If he was sober he would've known how lousy it made me feel to have him call me from a celebration party.

"Is Mountain there?" I asked him.

"Huh? That snob? Nah! Everybody says you shoulda made varsity. Mountain ain't crap. Hey, Roger— WHEEEEEW!"

He yelled into the phone. There was some scuffling, then we got disconnected.

I flipped TV channels for a couple more hours. Mom and Art came home. Mom was all bubbling and excited. She looked at me, and I watched her smile slowly fade. She tried to say something positive. But what could she say?

I went upstairs to my room. When I got into bed and closed my eyes, the first thing I saw was Mary Jo. I saw her long, slim brown legs and the way she bent her knees down low to hit those two-handed topspin backhands. I thought of her short white tennis dress. I thought of the way she had stood at the net, talking to Brock.

Then all kinds of thoughts and feelings gushed in at once, and when I opened my eyes and looked up at the ceiling, I realized my forehead was covered with sweat.

10

WHEN Monday came, I walked around all day telling my-self I was going to quit football right after school. But I didn't quit that afternoon. Or the next, either. I hung on, day after day, and I really don't know why. I guess Brodie had something to do with it. He just kept telling me to take it a day at a time and anything could happen, a spot could open up on varsity. But more than that, he didn't start trying to act cool around me just because he was hanging out with the varsity. He was pretty much the same old Brodie, and for some reason, that gave me hope. Anyway, I was first-string running back on JV, and for a guy who kept telling himself he was going to quit any day, I wasn't doing too bad a job.

Over on varsity, Paul Mountain was trading off with Hogness at running back and seeing a lot of action. I hated his guts.

As for Mary Jo, I couldn't figure her out. She wasn't all that outgoing toward most people, but she'd smile when she saw me in the hallway and usually come up and start a conversation. She'd mention that she hadn't seen me at the club and ask if I was playing tennis these days, or was I too busy with football? Wasn't there some day when we could play a set or two? I always had an excuse ready for her. After all, I'd watched her pound Brock and I wasn't in too big a hurry to let her know whether or not she could do the same to me. Even though I knew it wasn't too realistic, I also figured that if I kept her wondering about how good I was at tennis, maybe she'd develop some kind of infatuation with me or something.

Still, there were times when she'd smile at me in a certain way and I'd think she might actually like me. There were moments when I felt sure she'd go on a date with me, that all I had to do was get up the nerve to ask her. But that was hopeless, because whenever I came close to asking her out, my mouth would dry up, my face would freeze, my brain would go blank, and my voice would get stuck in my throat. And I'd think, You're fooling yourself anyway, you idiot. How could she possibly like you? This isn't the first week of school anymore, she knows you're not popular, she knows your personality's about as lively as a dead tennis ball.

A few days before Halloween, a note came for me in class. Mr. Parks, the coach of the boys' varsity tennis team, wanted to talk to me next period, during lunch. I found him in his classroom, eating at his desk. He asked me how football was going, and as we talked I wondered what he was leading up to.

"Rog," he finally said, chewing his sandwich, "I wanted to ask you something. Do you know Mary Jo Mountain?"

"Yeah, I've met her."

"Well, she came and talked to me this morning. She asked me what I thought about her turning out for the boys' team this spring."

I stared at him for a second. "Oh." Then I looked away.

"She told me she played Brock a few weeks ago." He smiled kind of skeptically. "She said she beat him all three sets."

I didn't say anything. I didn't bother confirming it or trying to act surprised or impressed or anything. I kept my eyes fixed on his desk, on the half-eaten tuna-fish sandwich that sat on some clear plastic wrap. Things were starting to make sense now; it all seemed to fit together.

"If it's true—" he went on, "and I emphasize the *if*—it looks like you, ah, might have a challenger this spring after all."

This time he waited for me to say something.

"Could be," I said.

He took another bite of his sandwich. "Anyway," he said with his mouth full, "I'd like you to play her."

I kept my eyes on his desk.

"What do you think, Roger?" he asked, wiping his mouth with a napkin. "Think you could do that for me?"

"Well, I'm kind of busy."

"You mean with football?"

"Well, yeah."

"What about a weekend?"

"I suppose. I guess I could play her some weekend."

He leaned back in his chair and looked at me. "You know, Rog, she and I talked for quite some time. We just chatted about the team, about the season, you know. I have to admit, I find it awfully hard to believe she could beat Brock at his best. Or you either, for that matter."

Mr. Parks wasn't a bad guy. I'd gotten to know him pretty well last season when I was number three on varsity. We'd hit together a few times after practice. I'd met his wife. I'd always felt like he was pulling for me.

I looked at him and wanted to tell him everything. That I had this gigantic crush on Mary Jo and I thought about her when I went to bed at night and when I got up in the morning. That I had fooled myself into thinking she liked me when all she wanted was to get me out on the court and see what she'd be up against this spring. And that being number one on the tennis team was about the only hope I had left of ever being a Somebody, and I didn't want to play Mary Jo because I wanted to hang on to that hope for as long as I could, kind of drag it out. But I didn't know if he'd understand. Even if he did, what could he do? Feel sorry for me? The coach of the varsity tennis team doesn't want to have to feel sorry for his number-one player. His number-two player, maybe. But not his number one.

"Listen, Rog," he finally said, "I know you've got football and everything, but if I were you, I'd play her." He kept nodding. "It'll be good for you to find out how hard you're going to have to train this winter." Then he stopped nodding. "She's aiming for you."

Mary Jo came up to me later that day in the hallway, as I was getting my notebook out of my locker. She had a friendly smile.

"How was that quiz in English?" she said.

"Okay." I closed my locker and started down the hall. She walked with me.

"Did Mr. Parks talk to you?" she asked.

"Yeah."

She had to hurry to keep up with me. "He's going to let me turn out with the boys' team this spring," she said. "If I'm good enough."

I gave her a quick glance. I wanted to ask her, What do you mean, *if* you're good enough?

"I think he'd really like us to play," she said. "I'd like us to play, too. What do you think? At the club sometime?" She waited for a second. "We could go have a Coke afterward or something," she said.

I stopped and looked at her. "You must really want to play me."

She smiled. "I'd like to see what I'm up against." She laughed kind of awkwardly after she said it. It made her face turn red.

I kept my eyes on her for another second, watching her cheeks color. Then I started walking again. She followed me.

"I'm pretty busy with football," I said, not looking at her anymore. "I don't know when I can play."

"Oh . . . You'll let me know?"

"You bet."

She stopped at her class and I continued down the hall, with no idea where I was going. I could still feel her watching me.

I ducked into the bathroom. I went up to the mirror and looked at myself. I had a look of total horror on my face. I turned on the cold water and splashed my face again and again. Then I leaned against the sink and let the water drip off while I stared into the sink. There was a giant wad of pink bubble gum in it.

I took some deep breaths. Staring at that wad of gum, I thought of the way she had blushed a minute ago and how I had almost broken down right there and grabbed her by the shoulders and yelled into her face that I was in love with her and I'd do anything to be with her—except play tennis. I closed my eyes and pictured for the hundredth time the way she had looked that day she stood at the net in her white tennis dress, talking to Mike Brock.

Then I heard the bell telling me I was late for class.

After school that day, while I was suiting up in the JV locker room, the JV coach came over and pointed at me. "Roger. Taller wants to see you. Pronto."

"Like this?" All I had on was my jock.

"Put some pants on. But don't keep him waiting."

I knocked on Taller's door. He was sitting at his desk. Coach Wills wasn't there this time.

Taller turned and looked at me, pulling his glasses off. "Coach Wills wants you to turn out with varsity this week. Zollenbeck has the flu. We've got a replacement for him at safety, but we need somebody with a decent pair of hands to catch punts. You're it. You're going to run back punts in the Mosswood game. Just punts. Got that?"

I nodded, because I suddenly couldn't talk.

He was already pointing to the door to show that the conversation was over.

It rained that afternoon. In the pouring rain and the mud I turned out with the varsity football team. I spent most of the time at one end of the field with our punter, practicing fair catches. By the end of practice, the undersides of my arms were sore and my face felt numb from looking up into the rain.

On the way home, I wondered what Mom would say when I told her I was finally going to be wearing a gold helmet. Sure, it wasn't a lot for her to cheer about, but it was something. Maybe I'd even catch a punt and run it back for a touchdown. Who knows? This was my shot, my one big shot. If I could run back a couple of punts and really show some moves, Coach Wills might just clear a place for me on varsity. It wasn't too late.

I wondered if Mary Jo would be at the game. She probably would, since almost everybody went to home games. Maybe when she saw me on varsity, she'd forget about tennis for a while and look at me a little differently. Maybe I *would* be different, now that I was going to play in a varsity game.

11

FRIDAY NIGHT. Halloween. If you're a little runt, you go out trick-or-treating. If you're too old for that, you meet a pack of kids at the shopping center or the school grounds, and you roam around. If you're a Clover Park Logger, you go to your team's football game. And if you're on varsity or just happen to be cool enough to get invited, you go to Bob Kortum's Halloween party after the game. I was finally going to make it to a Kortum party.

It turned out to be a rainy, windy, muddy Friday night, perfect for a scary Halloween but not the most ideal night for catching wobbly punts and trying to run them back. But I was ready. Well, I hoped I was.

We came out of the locker room to do our calisthenics. I can't tell you what a high it was to run onto that field to the Clover Park fight song, with all the cheerleaders jumping up and down. The whole school was up in the stands getting wild, and Mom, who'd gotten out of a Halloween dinner to come to this game, was sitting up there somewhere, trying to find number 23 in that mob of football players. She'd even talked Art into going.

We kicked off to the Mosswood Warriors, and with our team on defense, I started to get panicky right away, because I knew if fourth down rolled around I'd have to go out there and catch a punt. Half of me wanted that chance; the other half was scared spitless.

But the Warriors didn't punt that first series. They fumbled, and we recovered.

Next time Mosswood got the ball, our defense shut them down. Fourth down, fourteen yards to go, the Warriors had to punt. When Coach Taller yelled, "Punting Unit!" I took a deep breath and trotted out onto the field.

We formed a quick huddle. Kortum said, "Runback." That meant our defense wasn't going to try to block the kick; they were going to hang back and set up a punt return. For me.

I just barely heard the voice on the PA system:

"Roger Ottosen back to receive the Mosswood punt..."

It's a lonely feeling to stand in the rain all by yourself, looking at the backs of your teammates thirty-five yards upfield, not to mention the opposing players getting ready to stampede downfield and knock the crap out of you. Right then I really felt like the inexperienced sophomore I was, and I wondered why the heck Coach Wills had put a sophomore back there all by himself to receive a punt.

I stood and waited. I could hear the rain tapping on my helmet. Upfield, the punter held his arms out in front of him, waiting for the hike, and his voice, calling the signals, drifted down to me. The ball was hiked, the two lines collided, a thud, and this oblong brown thing spirals up in the air. It seemed to hover up there for minutes, although I guess it really must've been only about three seconds. I had to squint to see through the drizzle, and the bright lights in the stadium made the ball glow. I took a quick glance upfield and saw about fifty guys in white Mosswood uniforms closing in on me. Whether I liked it or not, I was going to have to call for a fair catch. I raised my hand and waved it.

Now all I had to do was catch the thing.

All of a sudden the ball plummeted like a wounded duck. I must've caught a hundred of those balls that week, but it didn't seem like any of them had fallen so fast. I took a few more steps forward, holding my arms out. The ball dropped into my arms. I held on. Mosswood surrounded me in case I dropped it. I didn't.

"Fair catch by Ottosen on the Logger twenty-nine..."

I trotted back to the sideline. Some of my teammates slapped me on the helmet. Coach Wills, with his headset on, was busy talking to the coaches in the press box and looking at his clipboard, but Coach Taller looked up briefly and said, "Good job."

We scored a touchdown that drive. Mountain crashed off-tackle from the three-yard line.

We kicked off to Mosswood with a 7–0 lead, and I tried to get myself ready for another potential punt. But Mosswood marched down the field and kicked a field goal. 7–3.

I paced up and down behind the bench, just to keep warm in the drizzle. Everybody was standing along the sideline with their parkas around their shoulders. There were puddles on the bench, with drops of rain splashing them. The reddish asphalt track that circled the field had a slick, glassy look under the bright stadium lights. Both the Clover Park and Mosswood cheerleaders were wear-

77

ing floppy rain hats and slick rain jackets. I looked up at the tall light towers and saw the rain shining against the black night. Last year at this time, I was up in the stands.

I'd been going to these games since second grade. More than a few of them were on drizzly Friday nights like this. Brodie and his dad and his little brother and I used to go to every Clover Park home game; we'd sit way high in the second level of the double-decker grandstands. The morning after the game, I'd lie in bed and imagine I was the halfback for the Clover Park Loggers. The players down on the field had always looked so big and old to me.

The first quarter ended without any more punts, still 7−3. But early in the second quarter, the Warriors were 4th and 8 on their thirty-nine-yard line, and the punting unit came onto the field.

In the huddle, Kortum called the same thing as last time: "Runback."

I was ready. I wanted that ball. But Mosswood never got the kick away. Their center snapped the ball over the punter's head. He turned around, ran after the ball, picked it up, tried to run with it, and got buried.

Our fans went wild. I just trotted back to the sideline.

My third chance for glory came with five minutes left in the first half. We now had a 13−9 lead. Mosswood was going to punt the ball from their thirteen-yard line.

This time, since Mosswood was fairly deep in their own territory, Kortum called for a block instead of a runback. I knew what that meant. It meant our whole defense was going to rush the kicker, so I would sure as heck have to think twice about not calling a fair catch. If we didn't block the kick, that is.

We didn't. It was a high, short, end-over-end boot, and I was a sitting duck unless I raised my hand and waved it like crazy—right now. I looked that knuckleball right into my arms and went down to one knee, while the white enemy jerseys crowded around me. Another fair catch by Ottosen, another round of applause by the fans, more pats on the back from teammates. I wasn't getting any glory, but I was doing my job, and that's all Coach Wills wanted.

During halftime, Coach Wills didn't give us a pep talk. He just talked about adjustments we were going to make for the second half. None of it had anything to do with me, but I still felt like part of the team. A couple of times I found myself staring at Mountain. I wanted to hate the guy, but it was tough. He sat there with a towel around his neck, looking at the floor while the coaches talked. His whole uniform was muddy, his face was streaked with dirt and sweat, and there was a big, bloody scrape on his elbow. His eye was swollen from where some tackler had stuck a finger in it. I wondered, If I had made varsity running back instead of Mountain, would I have been able to take that much punishment?

Third quarter. Mosswood punted twice. One of them was high and short, and I had to fair-catch it. The punter aimed the other one for the coffin corner, and I let the ball roll into the end zone for a touchback. Three quarters gone, and not a single runback.

By the start of the fourth quarter, we had stretched our lead to 19–9. That fourth quarter, it didn't look like I was going to get any action at all—Mosswood kicked a field goal and scored a touchdown; we scored another touchdown on a pass from Hiddleston to Dalquist and made our extra point. Adding it all up, we had a 26–19 lead with 4:29 left to play.

In the next series, their quarterback got sacked twice, and they ended up 4th and 23 on their own fifteen with all three of their time-outs and three minutes left. They didn't have much choice but to punt and hope they could get the ball back with time enough for one last drive.

In the huddle, Kortum said, "Runback. Don't touch the kicker. Don't even go *near* that kicker. And watch for a fake."

I stood back on the Mosswood forty-yard line. Taller waved to me to back up. It was pretty obvious he didn't want me to take any chances.

The kick was low and short. A line drive.

I knew the coaches probably wanted me to just let the ball roll dead. But it was such a perfect punt to run back. I couldn't help myself. I caught it against my numbers and burst full-speed up the middle, right through a gap in the tacklers, then cut to the left sideline and streaked. There was just the punter between me and the end zone. I saw him coming at me, a kind of dorky-looking guy, ready to throw himself at my legs to knock me out of bounds, and I knew just by the dumb way he had his arms out that I could fake him out of his pants. Sure enough, I gave him a stutter-step, he flew past me, and I cut back to the center of the field with my eyes on six points.

That's when the truck hit me. I felt my lungs cave in, and on my way to the ground the ball squirted out of my hands. I reached out, but I was falling away from it, like in a nightmare when you grope for something that's just out of your reach.

There was a scuffle for the ball, and the referee signaled that Mosswood had recovered it on their own ten-yard line, with 2:12 left in the game. I trotted off the field with my head down, hoping nobody on the sideline would bother to look at me. They didn't.

Mosswood moved down the field, tossing short passes and using their time-outs. Then, with forty-seven seconds left, our safety got called for pass interference on the three-yard line. It took Mosswood three tries, but on fourth down they finally rammed it over for a touchdown.

Their fans went berserk. Ours just sat there, stunned.

But we still led 26–25. Mosswood decided to go for two instead of settling for a tie. They tried a short roll-out pass. Kortum busted through the line and batted it down, incomplete. We ran the clock out and won the game 26–25.

When we got into the locker room, Coach Wills told us he wanted to say a few words before we took our showers. Things quieted down in a hurry.

Wills stood there looking at us for a long time. "We dodged a bullet."

That was all he said for about a minute. He seemed to look at every single guy on the team before talking again.

"If they had made that two-point conversion, we'd be out of first place." He shook his head. "We shouldn't have let ourselves get into that situation to begin with. There were too many mistakes in those last two minutes. The biggest mistake was that punt."

That's when he looked at me. I felt the blood drain out of my face.

"Now, you," he said, pointing, "you're a sophomore and you made a sophomore mistake. You should never

81

have caught that punt. There was no reason for you to catch it, no reason to run it back. *No reason to run it back!*"

He glared at me. It was the first time I'd ever seen him get angry. I looked down at the floor, wanting just to ooze into the bench, and it seemed like five minutes before he spoke again, more calmly.

"Well, we got lucky this time. But it didn't have to be that close. We can't afford the kind of mistake you made out there, son, not if we're going to be a championship team."

I took a long shower, closing my eyes and letting the hard spray drill the back of my head. Just as I finished dressing, Bob Kortum came up to me and put his hand on my shoulder.

"Don't let it bother you. Coach figures you've learned your lesson now. I don't think he'll hold it against you. Besides, we won the game, so you got off cheap. It's time for celebrating. I'll see you at my house."

I nodded at what he had said, but what I was most aware of right then was his hand on my shoulder. That was something I knew I'd never forget.

12

BRODIE couldn't get his dad's car, so we got a ride to Kortum's house with an offensive guard named Louie Loosha. Loosha had short, kinky black hair, foam in the corners of his mouth, and a laugh that sounded like a chain saw—*"Yeeeeeeeeeeeeah."* The fact that we had to ride with Louie Loosha kind of tells you that people weren't exactly lining up to drive Brodie and me to Kortum's party, even if we did happen to be on varsity. But at least we made it. Loosha charged us sixty cents each for gas.

The first hour or so, Brodie and I just kind of walked around and tried to act as if we knew what we were doing. The place was packed. We downed our beers as fast as we could and went back to the keg for more. I tried not to stare too blatantly at people, although I did my best to listen in on the conversations all around me, especially when Julian Hiddleston was charming a girl. Let me tell you, Hiddleston was smooth, suave, and sophisticated.

People in costumes started showing up from the Halloween dance at school. People from Hillside showed up, too—only the elite, of course. One of them was Mike Brock. Hillside had played an away game against the Vantage Indians and won 14–6.

I guess by the time Brock made his appearance at Kortum's, I was feeling pretty relaxed and cocky. I'd lost count of how many cups of beer I'd hoisted.

"How's the tennis game, Mike?" I asked, shaking hands with him like we were long-time buddies. I didn't feel nervous or awkward at all. I was feeling smooth, suave, and sophisticated. The question was, why couldn't I be like this all the time?

"It's football season," Brock said.

I took a sip of my beer and looked right at Brock. "I made a rookie mistake tonight," I said, shaking my head. "A dumb rookie mistake."

He shrugged and looked around. "Hey, it happens."

"Have you seen Mary Jo Mountain?" I blurted out.

That got his attention. He gave me a cool stare. "What makes you think I've seen her?"

"You played tennis with her once, a month or so ago. Is she really that good?"

"How good is that good?"

"Good enough to beat you."

He smiled, but it wasn't his usual effortless smile. "You'd better watch out for her this spring."

But with my beer in my hand, I couldn't help thinking that spring was a long way off.

I was going to say that to him. I was going to say a lot of things to him. I wanted to ask him all kinds of questions, like whether he'd gone out with Mary Jo and what they'd talked about and what they'd done. But he said, "Take it easy," and drifted off.

I stood there admiring him, watching how easily he

merged with a group of cool-looking guys who had mustaches and drank beer from Michelob bottles instead of Burger King cups.

I felt a tap on my shoulder. I turned around, thinking it was Brodie. But it wasn't. It was a girl, Jessie Bulmer, a sophomore. I'd known her since Mrs. Winfield's class in fifth grade. Back then she and I used to kick around a soccer ball during recess. One day, for some unexplainable reason, I ran up behind her on the playground and pushed her down on the cement. She started crying and went and told on me. That's about all I remember about our childhood friendship.

"Hey, what are you doing here?" I asked her.

"How ya doin', Rog!"

It wasn't too tough to figure out that she'd killed off a few beers herself.

She wasn't bad-looking, in a kind of frizzy-haired, tomboy sort of way. A little on the plump side, but pretty well-proportioned. She was wearing faded jean overalls. She looked different tonight and it took me a long time to realize that it was because she was wearing a ton of eye makeup and red lipstick.

We stood there drinking our beers.

"You see the game?" I asked.

"Nah, couldn't go. I had to take my little sister trick-or-treating. You suited up for varsity, huh?"

I liked the way she said "suited up." Not many girls would have said that.

"Yeah. I caught punts."

"Drop any?"

"Eight or nine."

"All right!" I watched her throat bob up and down as she drank her beer.

85

Suddenly it occurred to me that I was doing a pretty good job talking to her, and she wasn't acting bored or trying to escape. I challenged her to a beer-guzzling contest. The beer stung the back of my throat and tasted good. My head swam. Jessie's face looked fresh, her cheeks bright red. She giggled after she finished drinking. I kept my eyes fastened on her lips, that red lipstick. And before I could tell myself not to, I leaned over and gave her a kiss on the lips.

She made a face. "What did you do that for?"

"I felt like it."

"Remember when we used to kick the soccer ball?" she asked.

"Yeah, I remember."

"You were a riot in Mrs. Winfield's class."

"Winnie Winfield," I said. We laughed.

"Do you still goof around in your classes like you did in Winnie's?" she asked.

"Nah. I've grown up."

"You wanna sit down?" she asked.

"Sure."

"I'll find us a place to sit. You go fill up my cup before the keg runs out."

"Your wish is my command," I said charmingly.

Wow. She handed me her cup and I leaned over and kissed her again. We both laughed.

I weaved my way through the faces and bodies to the keg. I just kept saying something like, "Oh my God, oh my God, oh my God." It was the second time in my life I'd ever kissed a girl. The first time was at a party back in seventh grade, while I was slow-dancing with Paula Dennison. And now Jessie Bulmer was saving me a place on the couch, waiting for me to come back with her beer.

I waited for a couple of guys to fill their cups, then I held Jessie's under the tap and filled it up, then topped off my own. Some girl, dressed up like a punk rocker with orange and blue hair, a miniskirt, a black leotard, and black boots, came up next to me and said something, but I didn't hear her.

"What?" I said, turning around.

"Aren't you supposed to be in training?"

"Oh no, not you!" I said smiling, finally figuring out it was Mary Jo. I took a big gulp of my beer and looked at her miniskirt.

"Who's that girl you were kissing?" she said.

"Huh?"

"Your girlfriend?"

"What? No! Why are you all dressed up like that?"

"Um, I think it's something called Halloween?"

"Did you go to the game?"

"Yeah. We went to the dance afterward."

"How was it?" I couldn't've cared less how it was. I wanted to know who she'd gone with.

"Great."

"Was the band any good?"

"They were okay."

"Who did you go with?"

"Peter Mallory."

"Oh."

Peter Mallory was the junior-class president. He was what you'd call sickeningly preppy. I was drunk enough to say that to her. So I did.

"He's nice," she protested.

"Sure, you have to say that," I said. "Where is he?" I started looking around for him. I wanted to fight him right there on the spot. I wanted to be rude to his face.

She shrugged. "He's talking to somebody, I guess. He's always talking to somebody."

"That's because he's a prep."

"So that girl's not your girlfriend, hm?" she said.

"Jessie Bulmer? Nah!" Then, before I had a chance to think about it, I blurted, "We should play tennis sometime."

"How about tomorrow?"

"Yeah, yeah! Tomorrow would be great."

Peter Mallory came up. He was dressed like the Lone Ranger, all in white, except for a black mask. He looked at me, snapping his fingers irritatingly and pointing.

"Uh . . . Ottosen, right?"

"Who me?" I said, looking around. I wanted to be rude to him in front of Mary Jo.

"Riiiiiiiiiight," he said with a sickening laugh. "I think you've had a few too many brews, my friend."

"You're a dick," I said.

"Roger!" Mary Jo said.

Peter Mallory stopped smiling. He looked at me from behind that stupid Lone Ranger mask and I looked right back at him. I didn't back down.

Finally he pulled Mary Jo by the arm. "Let's go get some pizza."

Mary Jo stuck her tongue out at me over her shoulder as they made their way through the crowd.

My head was spinning, but it was only partly because of the beer. Damn, I was crazy about her. Damn damn damn.

I found Jessie sitting on the couch. She seemed drunker than when I had left her.

I sat down beside her and the next thing I knew, we were making out.

"I wish we could go someplace private," she said, out of breath. Lipstick was smeared all over her face.

"We could go upstairs," I said. "People have been going up there all night."

"Gee, I wonder why!" she giggled.

We kissed a little more. I tried different ways of kissing her. I tried opening my mouth a little. I tried poking my tongue in her mouth, and said to myself, We are now French-kissing. I forgot about Mary Jo.

The whole time I was kissing her, I knew this was it. We were going to go upstairs. Nothing could stop it now. All we had to do was stand up, go upstairs, find an empty room, and close the door. The thought of it suddenly gave me shivers.

"Ready?" I said.

"Yeah."

She pulled away for a second and blinked a few times. Her lips were red, but her cheeks weren't as pink as they'd been a while ago. She looked as if she'd forgotten something she was going to say.

"Will you excuse me for a moment?" she said in a strange voice.

"Where are you going?"

She didn't go anywhere. She turned away and very casually threw up in her lap. Brown liquid sprayed out of her mouth and splashed onto the coffee table.

That was only the warm-up. She lowered her head and started puking up the real solid stuff. Evidently she'd helped herself to some of her little sister's trick-or-treat candy.

"Are you okay?" I asked.

"Yeah."

Some girl I didn't know came over and helped her to

89

the bathroom, and some other girl started cleaning the coffee table. I just kind of quietly slipped away.

I stepped right on top of Brodie. He had fallen onto the floor, laughing. He was laughing so hard tears were rolling down his face.

Neither of us had any more beer after that.

THE WALK HOME in the rain sobered Brodie and me up.
We got soaking wet, but that was all right. We talked about
when we were kids. It took us an hour or so to walk to the
foot of the hill, where he turned off for his house and I
headed up to mine. By the time I had made it to the top
and cut across our lawn to the front door, it was close to
two in the morning.

The walkway leading to our front door was all lit up.
I stood on the porch, looking out at the street and listening to the soft sound of the rain and the loud sound of
water pouring through a drainpipe. I felt good. Deep inside, I felt just like our neighborhood, calm and content.
It had been good, walking with Brodie and talking about
the old days.

I felt kind of sorry about Jessie Bulmer. We'd have to
avoid each other now for the rest of our lives. I thought
maybe I should write her a letter or something, telling her
I was sorry I'd kissed her like that. Maybe that's what had
made her puke.

I had talked to Mary Jo. I couldn't remember much of what we'd said, but I knew I'd been pretty cocky. It was almost like we'd been flirting. She'd stuck her tongue out at me in a bratty sort of way, but I could tell she wasn't really mad. Maybe I was all wrong and she really did like me. Maybe tennis didn't have anything to do with it at all.

I walked into the house and felt a shiver. It was a good shiver, like you get when you crawl into bed. Since Mom and I had moved there with Art, it had never seemed like a real home to me. I'd never gotten a warm feeling coming into this house before, not like I used to get in the place by Empire Elementary. But now I stood in the hallway, and there was a familiar smell, like the house was starting to be lived-in, you know, like maybe a real family lived there, even though it was only Mom and me and old Art.

I turned off the hallway light. That's when I noticed a dim glow coming from the family room.

Mom was sitting on the couch. She was wearing the stereo headphones with the speakers turned off, so I couldn't hear what she was listening to. She was just staring into space, moving her head slowly up and down, with a strange smile. I stood there in the hallway, dripping wet, watching her. There was a glass of wine on the table next to her.

I took a few steps toward the family room. My wet tennis shoes squelched on the hardwood floor, but Mom still didn't hear me. She seemed so peaceful, the way I'd been, standing out on the porch looking at our neighborhood. I took a deep breath, wondering how I'd keep from startling her. Finally I went over and sat down across from her in Art's easy chair.

When she saw me, she didn't jump or anything. She

just smiled and kept listening to the music. Usually Mom is so hyper and everything, but for a while we just sat there together.

She pulled her headphones off.

"You're soaked," she said in a gentle voice. "I'd better get you out of those clothes." It seemed like a weird thing to say, as if she was going to undress me or something.

I stood up.

"Stay right there," she said. "I'll get you something."

She walked through the kitchen and disappeared into the laundry room. Music was coming out of the headphones. I went over to the receiver and turned on the speakers. It was "Hey Jude."

She came back out of the laundry room, carrying a towel and my old gray sweats, all neatly folded.

"Here," she said, handing me the towel. "Out of those wet clothes. How about some hot chocolate?"

"Okay."

She picked up her wineglass and took it to the kitchen and rinsed it out in the sink. I peeled off my soggy clothes and dried myself with the towel. I heard her shuffling around in the kitchen, opening the refrigerator, then the cupboard, while Paul McCartney kept singing "Hey Jude." I heard the whirring sound of the microwave heating up the cocoa. I put on my sweats, first the bottoms, then the baggy sweatshirt. It smelled fresh, just washed. Of course, Mrs. Wynn got the credit for that.

The microwave bell rang. Mom came out of the kitchen carrying two steaming mugs. She put them down on the coffee table, then picked up my wet clothes and the wet towel and took them out to the laundry room. Now the Beatles were starting in with the "Na na na nana na na" part of "Hey Jude."

I sat down in Art's chair and picked up the mug of cocoa. Mom had put a marshmallow in it. I took a sip. It was hot and chocolatey and good.

Mom sat down on the couch and held her mug with two hands.

"You played a good game tonight," she said.

I looked down at my hot chocolate. "Not when you fumble."

"Oh, don't worry about that," she said. "Do you think you might be on varsity next week?"

"I don't think so."

She nodded, smiling, and looked away.

"Did you have fun at the party?" she asked.

"Yeah, I guess."

"I won't ask if there was any drinking." She laughed a little, but I suddenly felt embarrassed. I wondered if she smelled beer on me or something. She must have. I hadn't even thought about that until just now. I probably reeked of beer. I took a big gulp of hot chocolate. It burned my throat.

She had her head resting on the back of the couch. She wasn't smiling anymore, but her face had a gentle expression.

When she spoke, her voice came out slow and soft. "I've listened to this song four times in a row tonight. Can you believe that?"

"Yeah, I guess."

She laughed quietly. "Your father and I danced to this song our senior year in high school."

I wanted to say something, but I didn't know what.

"This song?"

"Mm-hm," she nodded. "Once, one of his friends,

Jerry Bramwell, had a party, and we listened to 'Hey Jude' over and over."

"Didn't you get tired of it?"

"We never got tired of it. And now whenever I listen to it, it takes me right back to that night. It was a rainy night, just like tonight. And there'd been a football game, too, just like tonight. Almost nineteen years ago. God, has it been that long?"

I was glad the room was dark. I could see her eyes shining, and I thought maybe she had tears in her eyes. I wanted her to talk about my dad, but I didn't want to make her start crying or anything.

"Do you think Coach Wills remembers Dad?" I asked.

"I don't know. Has he ever mentioned him?"

"No."

"Have you ever asked him?"

"Me? Heck no."

"Well, I don't know if he'd remember or not."

"Did Dad like rock music?" I asked after a while.

"Yeah. Yeah, he did. And"—she laughed a little, it almost sounded like a giggle—"and country western. Ugh! I hated country western, but there was one station he *always* listened to. He *knew* it drove me crazy."

"Do you think he'd like the music I listen to?"

She thought for a minute. "Some of it, maybe. He liked Jimi Hendrix and Deep Purple and that sort of thing. So he just might've liked your music."

We sat there and listened to the song fade away. It made me feel good to think that my dad would have been the kind of dad who didn't mind my music. He wouldn't've always been nagging me about it and calling it filthy garbage, like Brodie's dad did. I tried to picture my

95

dad sitting around with me listening to my tunes. Every once in a while I'd let him play a country western song. He'd be a cool guy.

"It was fun going to the game tonight," Mom said. She still had that faraway look in her eyes. "Art and I sat next to Dr. Hiddleston. Dr. Hiddleston had a little flask he was drinking out of, and he kept yelling at the referees. It'll be fun next year. It'll be fun to get to go to every game and watch you play."

"You'll go to every game?"

"Every game. And I'll go to the football banquet with you at the end of the season."

"That's a father-and—"

"I know it's a father-and-son banquet," she interrupted. "And there's absolutely no reason in the world why I shouldn't be able to go. It's ridiculous in this day and age to have father-son anything."

She was losing her peaceful, gentle voice. She was sitting up straight now. I didn't want her to break this mood. I didn't want her to start harping about how sexist and outdated father-son football banquets were. I wanted her to put her head back against the couch and get that look in her eyes again and talk about my dad.

"Oh-ho. I'd just like to see them keep me away," she went on with her confident smile. "Oh, I'd love to see those old farts try to stop me from going to my son's football banquet." She thought for a minute. "Wait, JV can go too, can't they?"

I didn't answer. They could, but I didn't want to tell her. I didn't want her forcing her way and making everybody look at us, just to prove her point. She didn't care about my football banquet. She just wanted to show everybody how bold and up-to-date she was.

96

"Well, I'm sure it's for the whole team," she said. "I'm sure of it. You probably could've gone last year as a freshman. Why didn't we go last year?"

I just shrugged. I had gone with Brodie and his dad. Mom and Art had been at the Home Show up in Seattle.

"Well, I'll go this year," she said. "There's no reason in the world why we can't go this year. Father-son football banquets! Ha!"

I said good night and went up to bed. When I crawled under the covers I got a warm shiver. I thought of my dad. If he were alive, we'd go to the father-son football banquet, and Coach Wills and my dad would talk to each other about old times, and Coach Wills would tell me what my dad was like when he was on the team. Mom would be waiting for us when we got home. She'd fix us some cocoa and make us tell her everything that had happened.

I buried myself deeper under the covers and listened to the water pour down the drainpipe outside.

14

I WOKE UP the next morning with a gnawing in my stomach. Whenever I get that feeling I know I've done something stupid. It all came back to me in little glimpses—the football game, Jessie Bulmer, Mary Jo, Peter Mallory— and each flash made the gnawing stronger. The only thing that wasn't too clear was Mary Jo. I had a feeling I'd made a complete ass of myself with her, but I wasn't sure whether we'd made a tennis date for that weekend or not. I remembered feeling tough because I had stood up to Peter Mallory, but what came just before that had been washed away.

So, like the coward I was, I spent all weekend deciding to go to the club, changing my mind, then deciding to go again, and changing my mind again. How could I go there and face her? But what if she was waiting for me? But what if I showed up and she whipped me?

I didn't have much of a weekend.

Come to think of it, I didn't have much of a November. Football practices were cold and rainy and muddy. All November I hardly had time to pick up a racquet, except on Saturday mornings when I'd go to the club and play on the men's challenge ladder. Fortunately, I never ran into Mary Jo there. At school, she'd glance at me in the hallway, but she never said hello, which meant I'd stood her up that weekend after the party. She was probably waiting for me to make the first move, but the more I thought about her, the more I hid from her.

And I thought about her all the time. She'd pop into my mind at any moment: watching *The Three Stooges*, getting thrown down in the mud during a JV scrimmage, walking to school in the pouring rain. Or I'd be standing in the kitchen, staring out at our soggy backyard, and I'd imagine calling her up, or hearing my phone ring and having it be Mary Jo wanting to know if I'd like to go for a walk. I don't know how many hours I just sat around daydreaming about her.

Before I knew it, Thanksgiving was only a few days away. The whole school was gearing up for our last football game of the season, our annual grudge match against Hillside. It was always played on Wednesday night, the night before Thanksgiving Day.

Our JV season ended a week before Thanksgiving. We finished with a 4–3–1 record.

On Monday, two days before the big game, I had a shock. I was sitting in English, flunking a quiz, when somebody came in with a message for me. Coach Taller wanted to see me in his office right away.

"We're going to suit you up for the Hillside game," Taller said.

"You mean, to run back punts?" I asked.

"We'll see," Taller said. "Maybe we'll put you in for a few plays, let you carry the ball a little. You've had a good

JV season, you could use a little experience on varsity. You've earned it."

If that wasn't enough to take my breath away, what he said next was enough to knock the wind right out of me. He looked at me, smiled, and said, "Coach Wills wants me to tell you that he hasn't forgotten about you. He thinks you deserve more recognition than you've gotten."

I just stared at him. I must have looked like a complete idiot, but I couldn't help it. I don't know why, but the first thing that popped into my mind was my dad. Right then, I wished I had the guts to ask Taller if Coach Wills remembered him.

I wanted to ask, but I didn't. Hell, if I couldn't even ask Taller, how would I ever be able to ask Wills face-to-face? Maybe I was afraid Wills wouldn't remember my dad. Either that or maybe I was afraid he'd be shocked that Kevin Ottosen could have ended up with a son like me.

When I left his office, I didn't go back to class. I was too excited. I just walked up and down the hallway, thinking, "Coach Wills hasn't forgotten about me."

The hallway was deserted, since classes hadn't let out yet. There were signs plastered all over the walls with slogans like "Go Loggers, Beat Hillside" and "Shred the Papermakers." Hillside's nickname was the "Papermakers" because the pulp mill was over on their side of town. Other signs advertised the Clover Park–Hillside dance right after the game. Every time I saw one of those signs for the dance, I felt something like a knife twisting between my ribs, because I hadn't asked anybody and I was too chicken to ask the one person I really wanted to go with.

Well, it must've been more than a coincidence. I was looking at one of those signs in that deserted hallway when all of a sudden somebody came around the corner. It was Mary Jo. She was wearing faded blue jeans, a faded jean jacket, and pearl earrings, and her hair was hanging down over her shoulders, instead of being tied back the way she usually wore it.

Here we were alone together in this hallway, with me feeling a little confident, like things were maybe starting to click for me. I figured it was about time to take a chance.

I stood and waited for her as she came toward me. She couldn't very well ignore me. She said "Hello" and kept going. I caught a whiff of her perfume as she went by.

"Hey, Mary Jo?" I said, coming up to her. She stopped and faced me.

At that moment I think I came real close to doing something disastrous like throwing my arms around her. But instead I smiled, reached out, and gave her arm a little shake. Her jean jacket felt soft in my hand, and the scent of perfume was stronger now that I was close to her.

She got a surprised look on her face when I touched her like that, and she laughed. We both laughed.

"Well, what's gotten into you?" she said.

"Oh, not much," I said. "I'm just glad to see you. I—I've been meaning to apologize for—for not showing up that day. I guess I just...I don't know..."

"That's okay. Forget it."

"Are you sure?" I said.

"I'm sure."

I looked down and noticed that she was wearing brand-new tennis shoes. I tried to plan out what I wanted to say, but I knew that was hopeless, so I just went ahead and said it.

"I've been thinking about you a lot," I said. Then I started bobbing my head up and down. I felt my mouth go into a tight, weird smile.

"You have? Why?"

I wasn't going to bail out. Not this time. "Well, I've kind of been thinking about calling you up some time or something. I thought you'd probably hang up on me, though." I paused. "I'm suiting up for the Hillside game."

"Oh, Roger, that's great!"

She reached out and touched my arm as she said that, and kept her hand there for just a second. It gave me a little encouragement.

"I don't suppose you'd like to go to the dance, would you?" I asked.

Her smile went away. "The dance Wednesday?"

"Yeah. I know it's kind of short notice."

"Kind of short notice is right. Somebody asked me last week."

"Oh." I nodded. "Yeah, I'm not surprised. Peter Mallory?"

"No. Mike Brock."

Somehow I managed not to look like I'd just been slugged in the stomach. I just nodded.

"I might've gone if you'd asked me earlier," she said. "But it's too late now."

"Yeah. Oh, well . . ."

"What are you doing over Thanksgiving?" she asked.

"Nothing much."

"Well, let's make a tennis date. Saturday or something. Call me, okay?"

"Uh—okay."

The bell rang and the hall started filling up with people.

"And don't worry," she said. "I won't hang up on you."

I watched her walk down the hall. I was totally and completely in love with her and I felt like killing myself. I couldn't keep from thinking about her and Mike Brock going to the dance together, and I actually started to feel woozy there in the hallway. They'd drive around in his car after the dance and park somewhere and kiss. He'd casually mention that his folks happened to be spending Thanksgiving in Tahiti and his house was empty, and they'd drive back there. He'd have a bottle of wine waiting in the refrigerator...

I tried not to picture them together, but I couldn't help it. My body tingled all over. It didn't feel too good.

THE HILLSIDE football team, led by Mike Brock at quarterback, was crazed. They wanted us. They'd had a pretty disappointing season, and the only way they'd salvage any pride that year would be to kill us.

The whole week leading up to Thanksgiving, the two rival teams had been trying to psych each other out. One night some Hillsiders broke into our gym and ran off with Lumberjack Luke, our eight-foot-tall, wooden mascot. The next night some of our guys got back at them by ripping off their idiotic Papermaker mascot, which was nothing more than a big, grinning, stuffed rodent. We painted their parking lot with "Loggers Rule" and they painted ours with "Papermaker Power—Awwwwesome." Our principal and Hillside's made their annual bet: the head of the losing school would have to wash the winner's car. The rivalry was all pretty friendly and everything, but, I tell you, there was a heck of a lot of pride and tradition involved, and both schools considered this game bigger than the league championships.

And I was part of it all. I was on varsity. We wore our jerseys to school that week, and, in the hallway, ninth-grade girls who'd never noticed me before looked up at me with timid smiles and said "Hi." It was great.

The night before the game, I lay in bed trying to fall asleep, but the instant I closed my eyes, all kinds of horrible thoughts gushed in on me, like me fumbling the football and losing the game or dropping the winning pass in the end zone.

The next day there was a giant assembly at school, and the varsity players stood on the gym floor in green game jerseys while the pep band played the Clover Park fight song. When I got home from school I discovered that the pep club had toilet-papered my whole front yard and left a big sign that said, "Go Roger!" Mom came home early, at four o'clock, and made some spaghetti and garlic bread. She set three places at the dining-room table, with wineglasses and everything. Art opened a bottle of wine and poured some for each of us. Then he looked at me with his old-man scowl and said, "Give 'em hell out there tonight, Roger," and the three of us clinked our glasses together.

After dinner I had some time to wait around until Brodie came by to pick me up. I went to my room and stretched out on the bed. My stomach was so tense I had a hard time breathing. I closed my eyes and thought about Mom cooking dinner for me, and Art raising his glass and saying, "Give 'em hell." How did you give hell? It was just one of those things people said to you, and yet I couldn't help thinking Art had meant something by it.

Brodie's horn honked in the driveway.

I went downstairs. Mom was in the kitchen loading the dishwasher, and Art was sitting in his easy chair reading the newspaper. They said good luck, they'd both be there pulling for me. I swallowed and felt more than just butterflies in my stomach; I felt solid fear. For a second I stood there, wishing I could just be a little kid who stayed home with his parents and didn't have to go places. Then Brodie honked again and I hurried out the door.

Coach Wills made a short speech while the whole locker room shook from the noise of the crowd outside. We listened as he spoke to us in a low, calm voice. After he finished speaking, we had a moment of silence to gather our thoughts or say a prayer. I closed my eyes and took some deep breaths, but by the time I thought of something to say to God, the moment of silence was over, and everybody was up and yelling. We all gathered in the tunnel and stampeded out onto the field. The cheerleaders were waiting with a huge banner that read, "Loggers Have the Spirit," and we busted through it. It seemed as if the whole town of Clover Park was jammed into the stadium, one side with Clover Park fans, the other with Hillside fans.

The coaches had decided that both Zollenbeck and I would go back for punts, since the Hillside punter usually aimed for one of the sidelines. Our first punt return came early in the first quarter. In the huddle, Kortum said, "Runback." Zollenbeck and I trotted back to wait for the punt. I did some stretching, just to stay loose.

When the punt went up in the air, I saw that it was coming to my side. Zollenbeck shouted, "Fair catch, Roger, fair catch!" I raised my hand and waved it around and waited for the ball to come down.

Just as I caught the ball, one of the Hillside players crashed right into me. My whole body went numb and the ball popped out of my arms. I heard whistles, which I thought were coming from inside my head until I saw the yellow hankies flying all around me. Zollenbeck bent over and stuck out his hand to help me up. He was silhouetted against the towers of bright lights, and he looked like this big black object, sticking its hand out at me. I felt myself get pulled up, but my body wasn't too sure it really wanted to stand. My legs wobbled. The Clover Park fans were booing; then, as the ref paced off the fifteen-yard penalty against Hillside, they cheered.

My head kept gonging. I made it to the sideline and stared down at the grass. I thought, That's the first real shot you've ever taken in a varsity game. Welcome to varsity.

I felt a hand on my shoulder pad.

"You okay, Rog?"

It was Mr. Hill.

"That was a good shot you took out there," he said. "A cheap shot, but a good one."

I unsnapped my chin strap and looked at him.

"You okay, Roger?" he said again.

"Yeah."

"You sure?"

"Yeah."

"What day is this?"

"Huh? Oh. Let's see. Wednesday. Day before Thanksgiving. Clover Park, Washington, U.S.A."

He gave me a long, cautious look. Then he smiled, slapped me on the shoulder pad, and walked away.

After that, things got kind of weird, like my body and head weren't connected. I mean, I saw and heard the football game, I went out for some more punts and even ran one back for six or seven yards, but at the same time my mind was floating around somewhere else, thinking about things that didn't have anything to do with the planet Earth.

With five minutes left in the second quarter, fourth down on the one-yard line, Hiddleston ran a bootleg for a touchdown. Jeffers missed the extra point, and we led 6–0.

That quieted down the Hillside fans a little, and our side stood up for the fight song. I looked across the field and happened to see Brock, number 12, pacing up and down the sideline. I remembered that day at the club, way back on Labor Day, when I'd beaten him for the first time. I remembered how he'd shaken hands with me.

When I heard the gun go off, I just about jumped right out of my shoes. How could it be halftime already? I looked up at the scoreboard. Still 6–0. Where had the first half gone?

In the locker room, I soaked my head under the faucet, but my ears kept ringing and ringing, like there was an air-raid siren in my head. I said to myself, "I don't like football."

Brodie came and sat next to me on the bench and started talking. After a while he stopped talking and walked away. He had just carried on a whole conversation with himself. I hadn't listened to a single word of it.

I heard voices all around me, I heard fists pound against lockers, I heard the marching band outside on the field. The voices didn't seem to be talking in a language I could understand. When Coach Wills sat us down and started talking to us, I didn't have anything to do with it. What in the hell was I doing here? Why had I turned out for football? Why had I spent the whole damn summer killing myself running to the top of that bluff? For this?

I heard my name. I looked up. Taller was saying something to me. His lips were moving and noise was coming out, but I couldn't hear much of it. The locker-room lights were reflected in his glasses, so I couldn't see his eyes—they were just two glowing bright spots. I nodded. I kept nodding. Then he looked away and started talking to somebody else.

"PUNTING unit!"

Back on the field, standing on the sideline, I knew those words meant something to me.

The guy I was standing next to slapped me on the helmet and said, "Do it, buddy."

I looked at him. I saw the punting unit running onto the field. I ran onto the field with them.

In the huddle, Kortum said, "Runback."

I trotted downfield after we broke out of the huddle, and looked around for Zollenbeck. He wasn't there.

"Ottosen back to receive the Hillside punt..."

Wait a minute. Where was Zollenbeck? Maybe that had something to do with what Taller had been saying to me at halftime.

The two lines collided and the ball spiraled high into the night air.

"Maybe you'd better call for a fair catch," I said to myself. "Perhaps that's not such a bad idea."

Next thing I knew, the ball was in my arms, but I

hadn't called a fair catch. One guy threw himself at my waist, but he was going so fast all I had to do was sidestep him. I made a cut and shook off another guy. I ran another few yards before somebody finally tackled me by the legs. I hit the ground hard and landed on the ball. It smashed into my belly and took the wind out of me. I started gasping for air.

By that time somebody was helping me up. Somebody else handed me my left shoe, which had somehow slipped off.

When I got to the sideline, Taller led me over to Coach Wills, who was talking into his headset. Taller just stood there with his arm around me, watching the action on the field. Why was I standing here?

Taller glanced at me and frowned. "Hurry up and put your shoe on."

I looked down at the shoe in my hand, then bent over and put it on.

Wills said something to Taller. Taller knelt down as I laced up my shoe and said, "Go in for Mountain. Split-left pass 48 fake. You got that straight?"

I ran onto the field, pointed at Mountain, and stood in the huddle. Hiddleston looked at me, waiting for the play. I tried to remember what Taller had said. I had been so busy trying to get my shoe on that . . .

"Split-left pass 48 fake. You got that straight?"

Hiddleston gave me a look. "Yeah, I think I got it straight," he said sarcastically.

We broke out of the huddle. Dalquist went out split-left. Now all I had to do was remember what a pass 48 fake was.

I lined up to the right of the fullback. Yeah, that was it. I was supposed to drift a few yards to the right sideline,

Hiddleston would fake a pass to me, then turn and toss it to Dalquist on the left. Yeah. The ringing in my head was still there, but at least I knew what I was supposed to do.

I got down in my three-point stance. Hiddleston called the signals. My arm started to shake, supporting my weight. The ball was snapped and I took off to my right a few steps and turned and looked at Hiddleston. He pump-faked in my direction, and a stupid linebacker fell for it, ramming into my chest and knocking me flat on my back. He lay there on top of me, his face mask touching mine. His breath smelled like garlic. So did mine, probably. We heard cheering, and we sat up and saw that Dalquist had caught the pass and was flying down the sideline for a twenty-yard gain.

I trotted off the field and stood next to Taller. He looked at me and said, "Good fake. Stay right here in case we want to put you back in."

I didn't go back in for a long time, but that gave my head a chance to clear up a little more. Hillside scored a touchdown, but missed the extra point. The score stayed 6–6 for most of the fourth quarter. Then, with only 2:50 left in the game, Mike Brock connected for a Hillside touchdown, to make it 13–6, Hillside.

Our offense started driving downfield. On second down and eight yards to go, Coach Wills said something to Taller and then pointed at me. Taller pulled me toward him. "Split-left pass 48 fake. Got it?"

No way could I forget that play, the very first play I'd ever carried into a varsity game. I'd never forget it.

But the Hillside defense hadn't forgotten it, either. They totally ignored me and clobbered Dalquist for an incomplete pass.

Third and eight. Just over a minute left in the game.

I looked to the sideline to see if Mountain was going to come back in for me, but he just stayed next to Taller, who sent a lineman in with the play. It was the 42 draw. That was me, I was going to get the handoff. I should have been nervous, but I wasn't. Maybe it was because I had brain damage or something.

We lined up in the I-formation, with me crouching behind the fullback. Dalquist went in motion. Hiddleston faded back like he was going to pass and I straightened up like I was going to block, and at the last second he stuck the ball in my belly and I squirted through the gap in the middle. By the time two linebackers converged on me, I'd picked up a first down.

I went to the sideline. Wills was too busy to notice me, but Taller slapped me on the helmet and said, "Big first down, Roger."

Three plays later, with only five seconds left on the clock, Hiddleston ran a four-yard bootleg for a touchdown. That made the score 13–12. We were still behind. Wills and Taller started discussing whether to go for one or two points. I saw Wills look right at me, say something to Taller, look back at me again, and then signal to Hiddleston to call a time-out and come over to the sideline.

Wills looked at me one more time. Then he grabbed my face mask and yanked me toward him.

"We're going to do the 48 fake pass," he said to Hiddleston. He was still holding me by the face mask, but looking at Hiddleston. "Hillside will be expecting it. They think they've got it figured out."

"They do have it figured out," Hiddleston said.

"Be quiet and listen," Wills said. "They'll go after Dalquist. So I want you to do a double fake. Look to Roger, make a good pump-fake to the other side, to Dalquist. Then go back to Roger. He should be open. If he's not, you'll have to run it. Got that?"

"Yeah," Hiddleston said, giving me a glance.

Wills looked at me. "You understand what's happening?"

"Yeah." My voice cracked.

He kept his eyes on me. "Remember, the ball's coming to you after the second fake. Catch the ball, son."

We ran onto the field. Hiddleston explained the play in the huddle. "This ain't going to work," he said. He looked at me like he didn't trust me, like I was just some jerk sophomore he'd seen a couple of times who wasn't even going to letter this year.

I kept thinking, The ball's coming to me. Oh, Jesus. I don't want the ball to come to me. I'm going to choke.

The huddle seemed to last for ten minutes. My whole body was quivering. I felt dizzy. Suddenly I realized the noise in my ears had come back, pounding and pounding, stronger than ever.

I'm going to faint, I said to myself. I should call time out—I should go tell a ref or something—I'm going to collapse—I'm just a kid—I got brain damage from that first hit—I shouldn't even be out here. I'd heard of kids dying from football hits. Days after the game, some kid would suddenly collapse into a coma, his parents would sue the school district, and people would come and visit him in the hospital, only the guy would be in a coma so he wouldn't know how popular he had suddenly become. Eventually he'd croak, and his parents would get rich.

"On three," Hiddleston said.

We broke out of the huddle. I didn't clap my hands on the break. I kept mumbling, over and over again, "Please don't let me choke . . ."

"Set! Blue! Hut! Hut! Hut!"

I stood up and started drifting right. Hiddleston looked at me and pumped the ball in my direction, then looked over to the other sideline to Dalquist. That move sucked the entire Hillside defense to Dalquist like a vacuum. I was still drifting right. At the last second, Hiddleston looked back at me and fired the ball. It was a high bullet. I wasn't expecting it to come at me so high or so fast. I raised my hands above my helmet. I felt the ball hit my hands. It stuck there. A helmet cracked into my knees. I fell across the goal line. A referee was standing about a foot away from me and all I could see was his black shoes, but I could tell from the way he was standing, and by the explosion from the crowd, that he had his arms raised in the air.

Suddenly I was mobbed. The whole team unloaded off the bench. Somewhere in all the faces I found Brodie, with tears running down his face. I saw Mountain for just a second. Kortum fought his way through the mob and lifted me up in a bear hug. Hiddleston jumped on top of me from behind and we fell to the ground. All I could hear was a dull roar in my ears. I started to get to my feet. A bunch of my teammates had lifted Coach Wills onto their shoulders.

I made it into the locker room. We had to keep our clothes on while a reporter from the Clover Park *Chronicle* came in and got some comments from Coach Wills. We still had to keep our clothes on when our principal, Mrs. Guthrie, came in and congratulated us. It was chaos.

I took an extra-long shower. By the time I had finished getting dressed, the locker room had emptied out —most of the guys had headed off for the dance. Brodie had gone out to his car. I tossed my towel into the towel bin and turned around.

Coach Wills was standing in front of me. "Nice catch, son," he said.

"Thanks."

His face looked stern, like he had something more to say to me. "Your dad would've been proud."

Then he turned and walked away, leaving me alone in the locker room.

17

THREE DAYS LATER, on Saturday morning, I got up my courage—or went temporarily insane or whatever—and called Mary Jo. I guess I figured it was time to settle this whole thing one way or another. We set up a court time at the club.

After I hung up, I went downstairs to the kitchen, where I found Mom and Art having breakfast. It used to be pretty rare to find Mom and Art and me all in the kitchen at the same time on a Saturday morning. But lately it seemed we were together more and more. During the past three days, I'd been doing some thinking about Art. I kept thinking how he'd toasted me that night, and I wondered, hadn't he done things like that with his own sons? How could he have been such a failure with them?

He was sitting at the table with a screwdriver in his hand, scowling at the disassembled parts of the toaster oven spread out in front of him. The kitchen was filled with the smell of coffee, burnt toast, and Mom's perfume. She was dressed up in her business suit—Saturday was always a big day for showing houses. She looked sharp. She was bent over her toast, laughing about something that Art was grumbling about.

I took a deep breath. "Well, I'm playing tennis with Mary Jo Mountain today."

Mom stopped laughing. "Hey, she's a cute girl, Roger."

I had to look away, because I could feel her studying me the way she always does when she starts thinking about me and girls.

"You know, Roger, you should try letting your hair grow out a little more. No, now don't shake your head. You'd have naturally curly hair if you'd let it grow out instead of always pasting it down flat."

"Yeah, yeah," I muttered, looking down at the table.

"Really, Roger, you could be a good-looking boy. I mean it. If only—"

"Aw, let him alone, Connie," Art said. "Quit picking on the boy."

Mom and I both looked at Art.

"I'm not picking on him," she said.

"Well, hell, he wouldn't say so, even if he thought you were. He's too polite. You ought to be grateful."

"I am grateful," Mom said.

"Be glad he isn't on drugs. Half the kids these days are all hopped up on drugs." He shook his head. "It about floored me when I found out about my sons. Here I thought they were a couple of upstanding, all-American..." He shook his head, put the screwdriver down, and went over to the sink and leaned against it, looking out at the backyard.

Mom and I exchanged a look. She made a face and

motioned toward Art. Then she smiled and cleared her throat.

"Well, what do you know?" she said playfully. "A lecture about parenting from the Great American Father himself."

Art just kept looking out the window. I wondered what he was thinking.

Mom reached out and patted my hand. "You're a good boy. You know that. And you know what tonight is, don't you? The famous father-son football banquet." She still had that playful, mocking voice.

I nodded and looked down at the table. I hadn't expected her to forget about it, but I'd been hoping something would come up and she wouldn't be able to go.

"We're going, aren't we?" she said.

"Well..." I stalled.

"Oh, come on. I won't let you chicken out on me."

"Well..." I said again.

Mom's smile faded a little. "Well what?"

"Well, I've been thinking."

"About what?"

"About the father-son banquet."

"Don't tell me you're going to back out of this, Roger," she said. "I'm not going to let you back out on me."

"No, I won't back out. It's just that I thought—uh—I thought maybe I'd ask Art."

I don't know why I said it, but the minute I did, it seemed like a good idea.

Mom stared. Art was still looking out the window. I knew he had heard me, but he didn't turn around.

Gradually, Mom started to smile. "Wait a minute,

you're talking about *our* Art? The man who couldn't even..."

Her voice trailed off as Art turned around and looked at me. His lips were pressed together and his mouth was turned down sharply.

"You bet I'll go with you," he said.

A couple of hours later, I met Mary Jo at the club. She was carrying three tennis racquets, wearing flashy blue warm-ups, and had her hair tied back with a blue ribbon.

We talked a little, but not about anything special. I was curious about the Clover Park–Hillside dance; I'd heard from somebody who had been there that Mike Brock had been in a foul mood the whole night because of the football game. But Mary Jo didn't mention anything about it, and I didn't ask.

We started rallying. Her ground strokes were smooth and powerful and steady, and the more we hit, the stronger and steadier she got. I looked for weaknesses; I couldn't find any.

After about fifteen minutes of rallying, she walked up to the net and put her hands on it and leaned toward me with a smile. She knew she was good.

"How about a set?" she said.

"Yeah, okay."

We walked over to the bench and started peeling off our sweats. Neither one of us said anything. I felt my breakfast starting to creep up to my throat.

We walked out onto the court. I spun my racquet.

"Up or down?"

"Up," she said.

The handle pointed down.

"I might as well serve," I said.

My serve is my strongest weapon. I knew that if I could serve well right from the start, I could get some confidence. That was what I needed right then, confidence. I took plenty of warm-up serves, hitting them nice and easy just to get loosened up.

Then I held the balls up to show that I was ready to start. I bounced one and took some deep breaths, trying to relax.

I served and followed it to the net. It was a good, solid topspin serve to her forehand. She drilled it back, right at my feet. I scraped my racquet on the ground and half-volleyed the ball into the middle of the net. 0–15.

I served the next one to her backhand, and this time stayed back at the baseline to see what she'd do. Three shots in a row she chipped down the line to my forehand; the fourth, she blasted crosscourt for a winner.

0–30. I managed to win the next point with a hard serve and volley. At 15–30 I worked my way up to the net, she aimed her passing shot down the line on my forehand side, and I had to lunge for the volley. I missed it, and just about pulled my arm out of the socket. At 15–40, I double-faulted. So much for gaining confidence with my serve.

Things didn't get much better.

I was what you'd call outclassed. There's no other way to say it. She hit drop shots, she hit topspin lobs, she passed me down the line, she passed me crosscourt, she hit it right up the middle at my feet. Her stamina was amazing. There were points when I'd plant myself at the net, volleying her all over the court, moving her back and forth, thinking I was wearing her down and there was no way she could get to the next one, and then somehow she'd turn it into a passing shot or a topspin lob. When that happened, I wanted to take a bite out of my racquet and chuck the rest of it against the wall.

I lost the first set 6–3.

We walked over and sat down on the bench together.

"Want to play another set?" she said.

"Yeah, okay."

I wanted to and didn't want to. I wanted to, because I wanted to beat the crap out of her this time. I didn't want to, because I knew I wouldn't have a chance.

That second set, I could feel her let up a little. She let up because she knew she could beat me, and that was what she had wanted to find out from the very beginning, from the very first day she'd ever said "Hello" to me or smiled at me or tried to make conversation in the hallway. I had a 5–4 lead, but in the tenth game I could feel her start to put on a little more pressure. She was competitive enough not to want to lose the set. Sure enough, she started coming up with these amazing shots. The better she got, the worse I got. Pretty soon it was 5–5, then she broke my serve and led 6–5, and then it was match point. She put me away with yet another passing shot.

We went and sat down on the bench. I zipped the cover back onto my racquet.

"You're a little rusty from playing football all fall," she said. "You've sure got a strong serve."

I felt like turning to her and telling her to shut up and quit chattering. I hate girls who chatter just for the sake of hearing their dumb voices. She was gloating in-side—oh, boy, I could see that clearly enough! She couldn't wait to get by herself and throw her arms up in the air and run around and scream, "I'm number one!

I'm number one!" But what else had I expected? I had known this was all she wanted, ever since the day I talked to Coach Parks. But somehow I'd kept on daydreaming and fooling myself. Well, here it was, finally: reality.

"Come on," she said, "I'll buy you a Coke up in the lounge."

"I think I'll pass," I said, looking straight ahead and trying to control my voice. A couple of kids had taken our court and started hitting. One of them was wearing jeans. You're not supposed to wear jeans on the club tennis courts. I wanted to go out there and drag that kid off the court and beat his little freckled face to a pulp. If there's one thing that pisses me off, it's a couple of little runts out there just slapping a tennis ball around and not even knowing what they're doing. Just because their parents are rich or something. I could feel Mary Jo looking at me. I could feel my face burning.

"What's the matter?" she said.

"Nothing." I stood up. "I just don't want a Coke."

"Well then, how about a Pepsi?"

Oh, she was just in a great little mood, wasn't she?

"I've got to get going, really," I said, and started to walk away.

"Why are you acting like this?" she said, catching up with me. "You're being a baby."

"Oh?" I kept walking.

"Okay. If you're going to be like that. Okay, then!"

A couple of players on another court turned and looked at her.

"I didn't think you were a baby," she yelled after me.

"Well," I said over my shoulder, "I guess you don't know me too well."

"I thought I did. Boy, was I wrong."

"Well, you never know about these things. Now you know."

She hurried and caught up with me again. "Excuse me for beating you!"

"You're excused."

"Oh, just go away!"

"I am. You're the one who's following me."

"Yeah, well I'll stop following you right now. Good-bye!"

I just kept walking, out through the front door. I didn't really have any idea where I was going. A harsh, cold wind hit me, making my whole face go numb and my eyes sting. It was just starting to get dark when I ended up at Clover Park High. I wandered around the school and noticed there were a few cars parked in front of the cafeteria. They were setting up for the father-son football banquet. Screw that. Art probably didn't really want to go, anyway. He'd be relieved when I told him I'd decided to bag it.

THE HOUSE was all heated up nice and warm, and it felt good to come in out of that cold wind. I'd just stay in tonight and eat and sit around on the couch and watch TV. Mom had decided to work late since she wasn't going to the banquet, and now that I was letting Art off the hook, he'd probably go meet her at the office and take her out for a Saturday-night dinner. I'd have the house all to myself. I could wallow around. Maybe steal a few beers from Art's supply in the basement and have a guzzling contest with myself.

As I went upstairs, still carrying my tennis racquets, I heard whistling coming from inside the master bedroom. It was old-man whistling, the kind that goes up and down about twenty octaves, the way Bing Crosby whistles. The master bedroom was dark, but farther inside I could see that the bathroom light was on.

"Hey, Art?"

"In here, Roger."

His blue suit was on the bed, with about four or five

ties stretched beside it. He'd gotten out his old-man shoe-shine kit, too. I could smell the polish from the rags on the floor.

Art was standing in front of the bathroom mirror, shaving. He didn't have a shirt on. I'd never seen Art without a shirt before. His chest was kind of shriveled. His glasses were fogged up, and he had shaving cream all over his face. He was leaning real close to the mirror, shaving carefully.

"I was startin' to wonder about you there, pardner," he said, taking a glance at his watch. His voice sounded livelier than usual. "Go ahead and pick out one of my ties to wear, if you want."

"Let's bag it tonight, Art."

"What'd you say?" He turned the water down a little and looked at me in the mirror.

I was glad I was standing in the dark. He couldn't see my face.

"Let's not go," I said. "I don't really want to. I hate going to this kind of stuff."

He swished his razor under the water and turned around. He scratched his head and looked down at the floor.

"I, ah, I thought you wanted to go," he said.

"Are you kidding?" I was trying to smile, but the smile was all hard and twisted, and the inside of my mouth tasted bitter. "I hate all that crap. I hate getting dressed up like you're going to church, and having to sit at some big table with a bunch of people and eat."

"Oh..." He paused. "Well... I guess if that's the way you feel..."

I walked down the hall, went into my room, and shut

the door. It was dark but I didn't bother flipping the light switch. My digital clock radio read 6:41. I opened my closet door, threw in my tennis racquets, and closed the door. Then I opened the curtains and looked out at the neighborhood, at our front yard, at the dark, bare trees, their limbs being jerked by the wind. I felt a shiver.

I stood there until my breath had fogged up the window. Then I went over to the bed, dropped down on my back, and stared up at the ceiling without blinking. My mind started replaying that first set with Mary Jo, and I saw her shooting tennis balls past me, one after another, just out of my reach. Then I thought of after the match, and what a monster I'd been. She'd been shocked. She must totally hate me now. Good. That made things simpler. Now I could stop wondering whether she really liked me, and she could stop wondering whether she could beat me.

I closed my eyes and tried to shut her out. But then Art's face came into my mind, his fogged-up glasses, the patches of shaving cream, the whistling that sounded like Bing Crosby.

Suddenly I brought my hand up and slapped my face as hard as I could. It made a loud smack and stung me, making my eyes water. I tried to do it again, but this time my hand wouldn't obey. Half of me wanted to do it and the other half was chicken and wouldn't let me. I made a fist and pictured bringing it into my face, giving myself a bloody nose. Then bringing a fist down to my stomach and knocking the wind out of myself.

I wanted to make my body feel as much pain as possible, just to take the pain out of my mind. No, better than that, I wanted to do just the opposite. I wanted to get

129

drunk and go completely numb. I thought about putting on my football shoes and running the bluff. Maybe I could run so hard up the bluff I'd split my lungs.

No, the best thing right now was to go down to the basement and sneak a six-pack of Art's beer up to my room. I didn't care if Mom found out. In fact, maybe it'd be good if she did.

I tiptoed out into the hall. Art's door was closed. I could smell fresh cigarette smoke seeping out of his room. Well, Art could spend the night in his room puffing cigarettes; I was going to spend the night in *my* room guzzling.

I grabbed a six-pack out of the big refrigerator in the basement and carried it back upstairs in a plastic garbage bag, just in case Art happened to peek out from his room. Coming into my room, I noticed how much colder it was than the rest of the house. I flipped on the light switch and turned up the thermostat. Then I peeled off my tennis sweats, my shoes and socks, my shorts and shirt, right down to my jock. My skin got all goose-bumpy from the cold. I stood in front of the dresser mirror and looked at myself standing there with nothing on but my jock-strap. What a tall, skinny dork. I made up my mind to start drinking enough beer to get a beer belly. Yeah, a big fat beer belly.

I reached down into the garbage bag and pulled a can from the plastic holder. It was cold in my hand. There were beads of water on it. I gripped it hard and felt the cold go from the can into my hand and all through my body. Be a man, you wimp. I popped it open, brought it to my mouth, and started guzzling. When I pulled it away, I made a grunting noise. Some of it dribbled down the front of my chin. I felt like I'd drunk at least half the can, but when I peered inside it I saw that I'd hardly made a dent in it. I was going to have to work on my guzzling. I burped, looked at the can, took a few deep breaths, and got ready for the next guzzle.

My door swung open. Not even a knock. I must've jumped a foot. Art was standing in the doorway.

He was dressed in his blue suit, his tie tied, and everything. He looked me up and down with a scowl. I must've been a strange sight, standing there in just my jock, with a beer in my hand.

"Get dressed," he said. "We're going to that banquet."

"I told you I don't want to go."

"I don't give a rat's rear what you told me. You asked me to go to this thing, so we're going."

I started to say something, but he interrupted. "Now I don't want to hear any whining. Hell, my sons used to whine and whine, always get their way. Now look at 'em. They're a couple of bums."

"That's not my problem. Don't take it out on me, just because you screwed up with them."

"Maybe I did screw up with them. But I'm not going to screw up with you."

"What're you talking about? You're not my father."

"Well, I'm the closest thing you've got. Gimme that beer you got there."

He stuck out his hand. It was shaking. He stood there with his hand out, looking at me with that old-man scowl. His glasses magnified his eyes.

I handed him the can of beer. He looked at his watch.

"I'll give you ten minutes to get your suit on. You can borrow one of my ties."

He walked out and closed the door behind him.

. . .

Ten minutes later, I came out of my room wearing my brown pants and gray sport jacket, with my white shirt underneath, open at the collar. Art was downstairs in the kitchen, leaning on the counter with a drink in front of him.

"Where's your tie?" he said.

"You don't have to wear a tie to these things."

"Well, *you're* going to wear one."

"What's your problem, anyway?" I grumbled.

He just scowled at me. I took a folded-up tie from my jacket pocket. "I don't know how to tie these things."

"Well, come here, then."

"What for?"

"I'll show you how to tie it."

"Look," I said, holding up my hands, "I'm going to the thing, all right? I don't see why I have to wear a tie."

"You're going to have to learn how to tie one one of these days, so you might as well learn now. Come on over here."

Art stepped closer so that he was standing right in front of me, took the tie in his hands, and started pulling it through my collar so that it was the right length. I stood there letting him tie my tie. I felt like an idiot. He was bent toward me, breathing loudly through his nose, his eyebrows raised with that same squinty scowl that he got when he read the paper. I caught a whiff of after-shave, then a whiff of Scotch and cigarettes.

He finished tying and took a step back to look at it.

"Finally," I said.

"Just a minute." He reached out and started doing something to the knot.

"Come on, it's fine!" I said, shaking him off. "It's

hard enough to breathe as it is. I hate wearing these things."

"Hell, someday you might just have to wear one every day to work."

"Yeah, right."

I reached over to the counter and grabbed the can of beer he'd made me give him. I didn't really want it, but I took a swallow anyway. Art didn't do anything.

"Let's get this show on the road," he said.

A FEW COLD DROPS of rain hit us as we walked out to the driveway. It seemed cold enough for snow. The sky was a weird shade of orange.

Art handed me the keys to his Buick.

"You can go ahead and drive 'er," he said. "Careful, the roads may be a little slick."

We were just a couple of minutes late. The parking lot was pretty full, but I finally found a space. I put the keys in my jacket pocket. My tie was starting to choke me, so I stuck a finger inside the collar and pulled on it to loosen it a little. We walked across the parking lot. A couple of other latecomers were looking for spots. One guy's dad had left his lights on and was hurrying back to his car.

In the hallway outside the cafeteria, there was a group of fathers standing around talking. The sons were off in another area. As we walked in, one of the fathers saw Art and said, "Well, look what the cat drug in! Art Woods, you old dawg!"

He walked over and shook hands with Art. Another father looked at me and said, "How'd you manage to pull this old goat away from the poker table, huh?"

They all laughed. I shrugged my shoulders and smiled. Dr. Hiddleston, Julian's dad, came over and started talking to Art, and Art lit a cigarette. I saw Brodie and his dad, so I left Art and went over to them. They were sitting at a table, talking to Roy van Pelt and his dad. Brodie had saved us a couple of seats. I looked back at Art and saw that Coach Taller had joined him and Dr. Hiddleston. Art was amazing, full of life, talking and joking with all the fathers. I had never seen this side of him.

After dinner, Mrs. Guthrie stood up and made a quick speech. Then she introduced the guest speaker, Pappy Creeg, the retired sports editor of the Clover Park *Chronicle*. This guy was about eighty years old and had a million stories. He told us some stories of past Clover Park–Hillside football games. Most of his stories were humorous, but a couple of them were sad, and even though it was a father-son football banquet and you were supposed to be tough, a lot of fathers and sons and coaches had tears in their eyes.

When Pappy Creeg finished, everybody applauded him for a long time, and he gave a little salute and sat down at the long table on the stage. Then Mrs. Guthrie stood up again and introduced Coach Wills. He made a short speech, then started handing out the awards. First he called the names of all the guys who had lettered, and they walked up and were handed a gold C by Mrs. Guthrie. I applauded extra hard for Brodie as he and Mountain and the two other sophomores went up and got their letters. Then Coach Wills started giving the individual awards. The three most important awards were saved for the last—Captain, Inspirational, and Hardest Hitter.

The Captain award went to Hiddleston. Inspirational went to Kortum. When Kortum went up and took that trophy for Inspirational, everybody stood and applauded. Coach Wills told us that Kortum had accepted a four-year football scholarship to the University of Washington.

The Hardest Hitter award probably should have gone to Kortum, too, but it didn't. Maybe everybody remembered that first day Paul Mountain showed up at football practice. Hardest Hitter went to Mountain. As he stood up, I noticed he was the odd one at his table, and I realized that his dad hadn't come.

"And finally, I have a special award I'd like to present," Coach Wills said. "It goes to a young man who didn't receive a letter this year..."

Everybody started looking around the room to see who it was.

"We all underrated this young man. We didn't find out until the Hillside game just how big a heart he has. Even though he didn't make varsity or get a letter, he never quit, he always gave a hundred percent. So, a special award for Most Underrated goes to Roger Ottosen."

Suddenly everybody was looking at me and clapping. I teetered a little when I stood up. Art got up with me and patted me on the back.

It was a long walk to the stage, with everybody applauding. I finally made it up to Coach Wills, and he handed me a gold plaque and shook my hand. On my way back to the table, Brodie came out halfway to meet me, and we shook hands.

After the ceremony, while some people were hanging

around talking, I noticed Mountain standing at the pay phone, fishing around in his pocket.

I went up to him. "Hey, congratulations," I said, pointing to his Hardest Hitter trophy. "You deserved that."

I held out my hand. He looked down at it. I wouldn't have been surprised if he had just turned his back on me and walked away, since that's pretty much what I had done to him all season. But he reached out and shook my hand.

"How are you getting home?" I asked.

"My mom's picking me up. My dad had business in Spokane."

"Well, we can give you a lift home."

So we drove Mountain home in the Buick. After we dropped him off, Art told me to swing by the club. It was around midnight. I pulled into the parking lot and we went to the locker room. A group of men were sitting around a table in the corner playing cards. Art and I went way down to the other end, to a dark area that had benches where you put your golf shoes if you wanted them cleaned. It was deserted. I wondered what the heck Art was up to as he told me to sit down on the bench while he went away for a minute. He came back with two bottles of beer.

We sat there in the shadows for a while and sipped our beers. Occasionally there was an echo of laughter from the other end of the locker room, but it was dark and peaceful at our end.

"I wanted to tell you something," Art said after a while. "I wanted to tell you I knew your dad."

"You did?"

"Yes, I did."

"How did you know him?"

"He worked for me the last summer he was in high school. Back when I was in the construction business. Of course, that was before he married your mom. He was a good worker. A big, strong boy."

"I sure don't take after him," I said.

"Oh, you'll fill out. I'd say you take after him in a lot of ways."

"I do?"

He took a sip of beer and squinted his eyes and looked into the darkness. "You see, when your dad worked for me, he had all this steam built up in him. He was just a boy with a lot of steam to let off. By the time he got on at the mill, he'd done a lot of growing up. He would've been a damn good man. A good father."

Art looked down at his beer. In the shadows, his face seemed less tough and wrinkled.

"You know something, Art?" I said.

"What's that, Roger?"

"You're not that bad of a father."

He gave me a quick glance. We finished off our beers and headed home.

139

20

I PUT that plaque up on my bedroom wall, right above my tennis trophies on the dresser. Even at night when my room was dark, I could look over at it from my bed and see it there, just hanging on the wall catching some of the light from the streetlights outside. Most Underrated. Sometimes I'd wake up in the morning and look at it and remember how I had wanted to quit football, and I'd shake my head and smile.

During December, Mary Jo's face was real tan, the kind of fresh, ruddy tan you get when you go skiing every weekend. When I saw her walk down the hall I'd think of some tall, beautiful, untouchable girl in a bikini walking along the beach at Waikiki. She didn't do much more than glance at me and say "Hello," and I was surprised she even did that much, considering what a royal jerk I'd been to her. Whenever I saw her I'd just stare at her and hide like some kind of little wimp hiding from the school bully. Not even that plaque on my wall could make me forget how I'd acted when she beat me that day at the club, and I knew I'd probably never be able to say anything more than "Hi" to her, or do more than stare. And that made me feel lousy most of the time.

It also made me not want to think about tennis or look at my tennis racquets. They stayed stuffed in the closet the whole month of December.

The week after Christmas was cold and clear and sunny. You'd walk down the street and look up at bright blue sky, while at your feet there'd be mud puddles thick with ice.

Days like that always brought me back to when I was in sixth grade, eleven years old. That was the winter I first made up my mind I wanted to be great at tennis. During Christmas vacation, the days had been exactly like this, sunny and dry and frozen. Mom and I lived in the old house over by Empire Elementary School. We had just gotten cable TV, which included a nothing-but-sports channel, and for the first three days of Christmas vacation I watched a tennis tournament that was being played in Australia.

But one day I just couldn't take watching anymore. I remember it perfectly, the day I put on about three sweaters and a pair of gloves and a stocking hat, grabbed my old wooden racquet and a can of dead tennis balls, and went across the street to the playground at Empire Elementary. I started hitting tennis balls against the smooth yellow-brick wall of Empire's lunchroom. First I stood up close, tapping forehands against it from about six feet away. I made sure I could hit a hundred in a row before I switched to backhands. Then I moved back another six feet or so and did another hundred forehands and hundred backhands from there. Pretty soon I was all the way back to thirty-nine feet, the distance on a real tennis court from the baseline to the net. It took me all day to hit a hundred in a row from there, but I did it.

The next day, I went back and pretended I was the newest sensation on the pro circuit, playing John McEnroe in the finals of Wimbledon. I even kept score. I'd alternate between me and McEnroe hitting the ball, and I'd move that ball all over the wall and have to hit it on the first bounce. I'd serve, then start rallying, saying, "McEnroe—Ottosen—McEnroe—Ottosen—" with each stroke of the ball. I even came up close to the wall to hit volleys. I stayed there all afternoon, a full five sets, no tie-breakers. My arm just about fell off. I finally beat McEnroe, 4–6, 11–9, 7–5, 5–7, 6–4, just as it was getting dark.

The next day, Christmas Eve, I went back, this time for a match against Connors. My arm was so sore I could barely hold the racquet, and my hand was covered with tape and Band-Aids because of all the blisters I had. I figured out a new serve in that match. I discovered that when I served, if I used a backhand instead of a forehand grip, I could get more snap in my wrist and hit a good, hard topspin serve. Of course, it was kind of hard to tell just serving against the wall. I was dying to get out on a real court with a real net and try it, so I ended up riding my bike to the high school courts. Since I only had three tennis balls, I had to serve them, run over to the other side and serve them back, and so on. I stayed there till dark. When I got home, Mom was furious. My grandparents had driven up from Oregon, and Mom had cooked a Christmas Eve dinner, which we were supposed to eat at four, and here it was five-thirty. She was fuming.

But that night we opened presents. The first present I opened turned out to be a Head graphite racquet. I couldn't believe it. I was absolutely flabbergasted.

Thinking about that got me thinking about tennis again, which is what finally made me dig my racquets out of the closet on New Year's Day and start trying to figure out what I could do to beat Mary Jo this spring. I rode my bike over to Empire Elementary and stopped in front of my old house and sat looking at it from my bike. I kept telling myself: You used to live there. But it seemed a whole lifetime ago. Brodie's house was all dark; they were spending the week skiing. I coasted into the parking lot of Empire and found my old wall. Somebody had painted a line on it, three feet high—the height of a tennis net.

I unzipped my racquet cover, tossed it behind me, and started hitting against the wall. Nowadays, if I concentrated, I could hit a couple hundred in a row without an error. In that crisp air my hands were numb at first, but gradually they started to warm up. Pretty soon my whole body felt warm, even though my breath was still coming out in great white puffs and my nose was running. As I hit, my mind drifted. Would it be possible to beat Mary Jo? What would it take? How do you beat somebody that consistent?

Now I was really slugging that ball against the wall, putting all my weight into it. I could beat her. But it would mean working my tail off all January and February. It would mean running the bluff every evening, and using the ball machine at the club. And maybe talking Snapper into giving me private lessons. Dick "Snapper" Whitely was the pro at the club, the guy who'd hired

Brock and me to teach tennis last summer. Taking private lessons from Snapper would cost me a whole lot of money—the money I'd been saving up for a car. I'd be getting my driver's license in exactly two weeks. Which would I rather have: number one or a car?

Suddenly I felt this surge of energy. I hit the ball harder and harder. It echoed against the brick wall. I started playing a match against Mary Jo: "Mary Jo—Ottosen—Mary Jo—Ottosen—Mary Jo—Ottosen..." I beat her 6–2.

Okay, maybe I lost track of the score a couple of times, but who cares.

I pedaled over to the club, hoping that, by some fluke, Snapper might be hanging around on New Year's Day. He wasn't, of course, so I went to his office and left him a note telling him I wanted to take private lessons, and maybe he could let me string racquets or sweep floors or something to help pay for them. Then I went down to the practice court to use the ball machine. The place was pretty deserted since it was New Year's Day.

I plugged in the machine and started hitting some easy volleys. After I had hit all the balls in the machine, I went around, picked them all up, and reloaded them, this time setting the speed at the fastest rate it would go. At that speed, I only hit about half the ball supply before I was so exhausted I couldn't even hold my racquet, so I ran over to the machine as it kept spitting out balls, and turned it off. I sure didn't feel like picking them all up again, but you don't have any choice if you want to use the practice court.

While I was picking them up with the ball hopper, I

saw the lights go on way down at the other end of the building on court 1. A man and girl had started warming up. It was Mary Jo. The man had to be her father.

Mary Jo was wearing some maroon warm-ups that looked brand-new, and I figured they must have been one of the twelve thousand Christmas presents her parents had given her. She was standing at the baseline, hopping up and down on her toes as she waited for her dad to get himself loosened up.

What in the heck was she doing here? Why would somebody want to be here on New Year's Day, for cripe-sake? I finished picking up the rest of the balls, glancing at Mary Jo and her dad every now and then. She hadn't seen me, and I wanted to keep it that way. Her father, standing at the net with a basket full of balls, started hitting to her, quietly giving orders. He had a low, smooth voice that echoed across the deserted tennis courts.

When I finished picking up the balls, I went up to the lounge to watch them. I was the only one there, so I didn't turn the lights on; I just stood in the dark, looking out at the courts. Mary Jo's back was to me and her father was still at the net, facing me. He was making her do patterns—two forehands down the line, two backhands down the line, two forehands crosscourt, two backhands crosscourt, two forehand topspin lobs, two backhand topspin lobs. I watched as she repeated that pattern over and over and over again. She must've done it fifty times without a break. Finally, her dad ran out of tennis balls, so they walked around picking up the balls without saying anything.

After they had collected all the balls, her dad started hitting hard serves at her from the service line. He only paused from serving long enough to grab a new handful of tennis balls. Some of his serves came at her so fast she could hardly get out of the way of the ball, much less hit it, and one time her arms got tied up and the ball smacked her right in the stomach. She doubled over. Her father lowered his racquet.

"Okay?" he said.

"Yeah."

She straightened back up and her father started serving at her again.

After a while she was able to react fast enough to those serves to get her racquet on them. After a few more she could block them down the line with her backhand. Pretty soon she was hitting hard topspin returns to either side of the court.

I stood there in the dark, watching her. Her father hit serve after serve; she hit return after return. And I knew that if she hit returns like that against me as I was coming to the net, I wouldn't have a chance. Not a chance in hell.

21

A FEW DAYS later, Snapper called me up about the lessons and told me to come see him after school to talk about it.

His office at the club was small and cluttered with all kinds of weird objects—photographs, socks, trophies, old tournament drawsheets. On one wall was a picture of him in a suit and tie, standing next to Arthur Ashe. It was autographed by Ashe. Another photo was of Snapper shaking hands at the net with Bjorn Borg after Borg had beaten him in the third round of the French Open, 6–3, 6–3, 6–3. Snapper always joked about how that was his greatest moment. On his messy desk was a calendar with a half-naked girl, a swamp of papers, and old crusty Whopper boxes from Burger King. In the middle of all that was a picture of his two little sons.

Sitting behind his desk in his tennis sweats, Snapper looked at me for a long time without saying anything. His cheeks were always bright red, as if he was angry or embarrassed about something.

"Why private lessons?" he asked, tipping back in his squeaky wooden chair. "Isn't the Junior League good enough for you?"

I told him I wanted to make sure I made number one that spring.

"Oh, yeah?" he laughed. "Mary Jo's got you a little nervous, that it?"

"Yeah."

His smile faded a bit. My honesty had surprised him. I think he'd always figured me as being a smart-ass.

"Listen, Rog, I'll be straight with you. I've hit with that gal. She's right on the ball, steady as they come. You want to beat her? You're going to have to reach down inside yourself, my man." He shook his head. "You're a good player, but you've always reminded me of Brock. You and Brock rely too much on being natural athletes. You guys have never had to work. You've never been challenged. I mean, look at you." He held out his hand and looked me up and down. "Have you ever had to work for anything? I mean, really work?"

I didn't answer. I didn't know whether he wanted me to answer or not, and to tell you the truth, I didn't know what the answer was.

He went on, shaking his head slowly, and smiling as he spoke. "Everything's *given* to you, man. You and Brock. You got your rich mommies and daddies. They let you join the tennis club. You play tennis now and then when you feel like it. Nobody in this town can beat you. You're natural athletes. Easy. So last June I ask you if you might want to test yourself a little, try some tournaments in eastern Washington over the summer. '*Well, gee, I don't know, I've got football and everything.*'"

He was mimicking the way he thought I sounded,

tipping his head left and right, with a bratty look on his face.

"Now, me," he said, "I had to work my way up the hard way. My parents didn't have any dough. I had to scrape along on public courts. I had to work my buns off, man. Have you ever had a real job? The only job you've ever had is the one I gave you last summer, teaching tennis. Some job. Brock puts the hustle on the teeny-boppers and you play games with the kiddies." He kept his eyes on me, shaking his head. "So you finally found out life's not so easy, that it? You're going to be challenged by that gal, and you're scared. That it?"

"I guess."

"You planning on coming back this summer to work for me?"

"Yeah, if you'll let me."

He exhaled a long breath. "Okay. We'll make a deal. I start giving you lessons now, you pay me as much as you can, and I'll take the rest out of your paycheck this summer. How's that sound?"

"That sounds good, Snapper."

"But I'm warning you. I'm gonna push you. You understand?"

"Yeah."

"So how often do you want to come in? Three days a week? Or you think you want to go for four?"

"Four. Four would be great."

"Well, it's up to you. I'll help you as much as I can, but it's up to you. I don't want you skipping out on me, missing lessons and making excuses and all that. If you pull that crap on me, I'll say forget it. It's got to be all or nothing. Like I say, you're going to have to reach inside yourself if you want to beat her."

I nodded.

He thought for a minute, and a smile came to his face. "You know something? If you beat her, you'll *kill* Brock. But the question is, can you beat that gal?"

I asked myself that question about a million times in the next two months. When I ran the bluff in the freezing cold, and when I worked out on weights at the club to try to build up some strength and stamina, and when I went to bed or got up in the morning and looked at that plaque on my wall.

I saw Mary Jo a lot at the club. She knew I was taking private lessons from Snapper. Sometimes I'd see her watching me. She'd be hitting on the ball machine, or playing against one of the club members, or practicing with her father, and I'd catch her watching me doing drills with Snapper. Drills, drills, drills. Volleying drills, overhead drills, half-volley drills, approach-shot drills, accuracy drills, reflex drills. Mary Jo must've known that all those drills were for her.

One day in February, after a workout, I went up to the lounge to get a Coke, and there she was, almost like she'd been waiting for me. We were alone. I made a big deal about fishing around for some change in my pocket and selecting my Coke from the vending machine. I could feel her eyes on me. She was facing me, with her back to the tennis courts, sitting on one of the tables that was pushed up against the viewing window. She was wearing a kind of ragged, dark blue sweatshirt unzipped part of the way down the front, with the blue Seahawks T-shirt and white running shorts that she'd worn the first day I saw her, on the track before football practice. Her arms were crossed, and the baggy sleeves of her sweatshirt were pushed up to her elbows.

When I took my Coke out of the machine and turned around, she was looking right at me. "I don't see why we can't hit together every once in a while," she said.

I looked away real fast as I took a swig of my Coke.

She sat on that table, her long bare legs stretched out in front of her, her arms still crossed, her sleeves rolled up, showing off those forearms with their little blond hairs. I wanted to say, "Why do you even bother talking to me? You must really want to see how much I've improved these last few weeks. Maybe I *was* just rusty from football, that time we played. You're not sure, are you? You want to check me out. Well, you don't have to be so sneaky about it." But I kept my mouth shut.

I walked over by the window and stood next to her, and looked out at some ladies playing doubles. They were all wearing white tennis dresses. One of the ladies was real old—her legs were tanned and wrinkled.

"I mean, we're not enemies," she said, looking at me. "I don't see why we can't help each other out a little bit."

I was still looking out the viewing window, but from the corner of my eye I could see her long, slender legs, and I got that woozy feeling I'd gotten so many times thinking about her and watching her. She was the kind of girl you look at and say, "I'll never have anybody like that. Not me."

"We could practice together sometimes or something," she said.

I shrugged. "Why?"

"So we could both get better."

"You always practice with your father."

153

"Not always. He's out of town a lot. Besides, it'd be fun to practice with—with somebody like you. I don't get you, Roger. This isn't all that easy for me, you know."

I didn't say anything for a while. I could hear the echoes of racquets hitting tennis balls, coming from the courts below.

"I feel pretty bad about the way I acted that day," I finally said.

"Oh, forget about that. I shouldn't have gotten so mad."

"Sure you should've," I said, "of course you should've. The thing is—it's just that I've always wondered what it would be like if we didn't both happen to play tennis. You know, like if I just called you up or something."

"I don't see why you haven't," she said.

"Haven't what?"

"Called me up. Have I ever not been friendly to you?"

"No. But I always thought, if it wasn't for the fact that I'm number one on the tennis team, and you're going to be challenging me, you never would have . . ."

"Never would have what?"

I shook my head.

She stared at me. "Never would have bothered talking to you? Jeesh! You give me a lot of credit, don't you? I happen to think you're a lot nicer than most of the boys I've met in this town. And you can either believe that or not, whichever you like."

"I'm actually not as bad as I act around you," I said, kind of perking up. Then I hesitated and took a deep breath. "Do you—do you ever go bowling or anything?"

"Bowling?"

"Yeah. It's pretty fun, actually. There's this thing called Red Pin Nite. You can win money."

"I haven't bowled for about a year. You'd probably cream me."

"So what? You never know. Sometimes you pick up a ball and it comes right back to you. Bowling, I mean—not the ball."

"Are you very good?" she asked.

"Ha! Are you kidding? I'm lousy...Oh, I'm not that bad, I guess."

"I bowled a 186 once," she said. "That's my highest score."

"You're kidding. 186? That's great."

"Red Pin Nite, huh? I guess it could be fun."

"Yeah, it really is. It's on Friday and Saturday nights." I nodded. "You have to call up and reserve a lane." I kept nodding. "I could call up and reserve one sometime, if you want. You can always cancel."

"Okay."

"Like I say, you can always cancel. How about this Friday—unless you'd rather go Saturday."

"No, let's go Friday."

"Okay." I still kept nodding. I didn't know how it had happened, but I felt pretty good. I felt like our conversation should end now before I did something to foul it up.

"Well," I said, "I'd better take off. I'll let you know. At school. If you want to cancel, just let me know."

"Okay."

I finished off my Coke and tossed the can into the recycling bin on my way out of the lounge.

AFTER THAT, everything seemed to happen like in a dream. In a dream, you can just barely remember what happens, but you can't explain why or how. You can't really get down to specific details or anything. The minute you wake up, it fades, and you start to forget.

We went bowling that Friday night. The place was packed. Cigarette smoke everywhere. I didn't get my first shot at a red headpin till the sixth frame. I took careful aim, went into my four-step approach, released the ball smoothly, followed through, and—bam! Strike! It was the first time I'd ever hit a ten-dollar shot on Red Pin Nite: usually I just won fifty cents or a buck or something. When I hit that strike, I heard Mary Jo scream. She actually screamed, but at least she didn't run up to me and start yelling "Goodie, goodie!" I knew she wasn't the kind of girl who'd do a thing like that, and she didn't. People in the lanes next to us clapped and said, "Way to go!" That's the good thing about Red Pin Nite: everybody's happy for you when you hit a money shot. You feel like you're at a big party where everybody's having fun and rooting for you. Bowlers are good people. They smoke a lot of cigarettes, but they're good people.

Mom had let me use her Volvo, so after the bowling, we pulled up in front of Mary Jo's house and sat in the car. After a few minutes, I said, "Do you want to just drive around a little?" We went over to my old neighborhood and I showed her where I used to live and the wall I used to hit tennis balls against. I showed her the cemetery where my dad's buried, and we drove past the mill where he was killed. By the time we got back to her house, we were all talked out, so for a minute there was a kind of comfortable silence. When she finally said good night, I watched her walk to her front door, and I just kept shaking my head and saying to myself, "This is me taking her home from a date. Not Brock or Hiddleston or Peter Mallory. What do you know about that?"

The next Friday night, my mom gave me two Sonics tickets that her office usually held for clients, and Mary Jo and I made a date to drive up to Seattle and watch the game. Mom gave me some money to take Mary Jo out to dinner with, and she kept telling me all this stuff about how big a tip to leave and all that, like she was going to give me a quiz on it or something, but I could tell she was thrilled, really thrilled, and that made me feel good.

I had to go in and meet Mary Jo's father and mother and shake hands with them and make conversation and all that. It was hell. Her dad looked me up and down with a sharp, critical eye, and I wasn't sure whether he was looking at me as his daughter's date or as the guy he and his daughter were practicing to beat that spring.

We went bowling two or three more Friday nights.

Once Mary Jo bowled a 200 game. She was one of those people who are just naturally good at whatever sport they try, and who always, *always,* play to win. One cold Friday night we went downstairs to her rec room and played eighteen straight games of Ping-Pong. She won 10–8. Sweat was pouring down our faces.

Brodie came over to my house a lot during that time, and no matter what we did, we always seemed to end up talking about the same thing. He'd ask me all kinds of detailed questions about what Mary Jo and I did—not because he was nosy, but because he really wanted to know what going out with a girl was like. When he'd end up feeling sorry for himself for never having a girl to go out with, I found myself telling him the same sorts of things he'd told me back in the fall—just hang in there and take it a day at a time, anything can happen. I was proof of that.

I continued taking my lessons with Snapper, and sometimes Mary Jo would watch me, or I'd watch her hit with her dad, and we'd have a Coke together up in the lounge. But we didn't play tennis against each other, not once. We knew how competitive we both were, so we avoided it. Ping-Pong, yes; tennis, no.

That is, until the first weekend in March, just three weeks before tennis tryouts were to start. It was one of those days in early March when you can smell spring in the air. It was such a nice day that Mary Jo and I decided it wouldn't hurt to drive over to the high school courts and hit some tennis balls outside.

It turned out that a lot of other people had the same idea—all eight courts were taken, and there were people waiting to get on. There were even people just sitting up in the bleachers, watching the tennis and enjoying the

159

sun. We weren't in any hurry, so we walked past the bleachers and up the grassy hill that overlooked the courts. We stretched out in the sun with our hands behind our heads and looked up at the blue sky.

Mary Jo raised herself up on her elbow and looked down at me, and, like it was the most natural thing in the world, she leaned over and kissed me.

"Roger?"

"Yes?"

"Do you think about it very much? That I'm going to be challenging you?"

"Yes."

"What do you think?"

"I don't know. What do you think?"

"I think I feel a lot of pressure. I know that's stupid, but I do."

"It's not stupid," I said. "It's hard to be friends when you feel that pressure. It's hard not to think you're my enemy."

She looked away. She was still leaning over me, but her mind was somewhere else.

I studied her face. It was a perfect, perfect face.

She looked back at me. "Roger?"

"Yes?"

She brightened, like an idea had come to her. "I don't see why we can't be friends no matter what. We should be able to be friends, don't you think? I mean, it's stupid to be that way. We shouldn't let tennis wreck it."

"You're right about that," I said.

"Yes, I am. We'll just have to stick together, that's all. We can't be enemies. Of course, that's easy to say, if you happen to be the one who wins. But when you lose, *that's* the thing. It's up to the loser, you know."

"You mean it's up to the loser not to act like I acted," I said.

She laughed, and when I saw her laugh like that, her face all lit up and everything, well, I don't know, I know it sounds corny, but lying there on the grass next to her, I could feel life and love all around me. Everything was so alive and real, like it was all radiating from her face. The grass had never looked greener or felt softer. The branches of the trees were still bare, but you could see they'd be coming back to life pretty soon. The breeze swishing through the evergreens sounded like a waterfall. I wanted to burst out laughing and crying at the same time.

We looked up at the clouds and saw a plane way up high, heading west. As we watched it disappear, I thought, Clover Park is the most beautiful place in the world.

When we finally got up and headed back down the hill, the courts were still full, so we decided to bag the tennis after all. We walked by the last court where a guy and a girl about college age were playing. We stopped to watch them for a minute. Then the college guy turned around and smiled and said, "You guys want our court?"

Mary Jo and I looked at each other, and gave a little nod.

And just like that, we were out on the court hitting, while the college guy and girl sat on the bench watching us. I knew how good we must have looked to them, how beautiful Mary Jo was and how unbelievable her tennis strokes were as she stood on the baseline rallying with me.

That's when it hit me. All those times I'd sat on the bluff dreaming this very scene . . . It was happening here

161

and now, right down to the sunny day with the smell of spring in the air, the pleasant people letting us have their court and admiring us as we hit. How many times had I thought of this and said to myself, "If I had that, I'd be happy. Nothing else would matter. Nothing at all—football, tennis, parties, Kortum, Hiddleston, Brock..."

I guess maybe for a second I actually thought I was back up on the bluff with my eyes closed, fantasizing the whole thing. I know that sounds impossible, but no more impossible than realizing that the fantasy had actually come true. Imagine dreaming about something for so long, and suddenly finding yourself right in that dream —everything seems real, but you've spent so much time dreaming it that you can't believe it could really be happening. It's confusing, and scary, because if you think about it long enough, you don't know what's real at all.

It's amazing what your body can do when your mind's not in the way. I wasn't even thinking about hitting the ball, and for that reason I was hitting perfect shots. The ball looked big and clear to me, the racquet felt like an extension of my arm, and the strings seemed to catch hold of the ball and give it any kind of spin I wanted.

We started to press each other a little and pick up the pace on the rally. Pretty soon we were hitting everything on only one bounce, really hustling for each ball. Mary Jo hit a few casual serves, and I started returning them, and pretty soon we were playing points, without keeping score.

Then she smiled and said, "Oh, heck, how about a set?"

"Sounds okay to me," I said.

So we started keeping score.

We had long, close games. Back and forth, from deuce to advantage, back to deuce. We got more intense with each game—but it was also the most fun I'd ever had playing tennis.

She stayed back on the baseline and played her steady, consistent game, and I attacked the net. My volleys were sharp, my ground strokes were harder and more accurate than they'd ever been. I could aim for the deep corner and hit it. I could shoot the ball right down the line, or chip it crosscourt at a sharp angle. I tell you, I couldn't miss. I moved her all around, left and right, choosing the right time to move to the net, then anticipating her passing shot or lob, and putting it away, just like that. All those drills with Snapper were paying off. But there was more to it than that. There was something different about me. I'd never concentrated like this before. Everything was so simple—there was no challenge match coming up, no number one, no winning or losing; there was just a tennis ball that needed to be hit as perfectly as it could be.

I won that set 6–4. It took us almost an hour.

We played another. We were both sweating, even though by now we were playing in the glow of sunset. The air was really starting to get a bite to it, and I remembered that it wasn't even spring. It was still late winter, March. It had all been an illusion. Spring, love, everything. The bleachers were empty, the people were gone. The trees looked dark, bare, and dead. I wanted to beat Mary Jo and she wanted to beat me, and that was about all there was to it.

We finished that set with the lights on. I won 6–3.

We sat down on the bench. I watched her zip up her

racquet cover. She wouldn't look at me. Her lips were pressed tightly together. The night air was crisp and cold and I could see my breath.

"Well," she said, "good game."

That was all she said. She stood up.

I just sat on the bench with my elbows on my knees, looking at the ground.

"I don't know," I said, shaking my head.

"What don't you know?"

"I guess maybe it was pretty dumb to think we could be friends."

"I don't know either," she said, looking out at the courts. "I don't know what I think. I think I want to be number one. I hate to lose. I won't lose." She paused and let out a sigh. "But maybe when all this is over..."

I laughed, but I don't know why. It didn't feel good.

"I know what you're talking about," I said. "That's what I thought, too, that I just wanted to win and be number one. That's what I've always thought. Except, you know what? About an hour ago, that's the best tennis I've ever played in my whole life. And you know why? Because I didn't care anymore."

"About what?"

"About any of this. All the stuff I wanted: being number one in tennis, and varsity in football, and—and —having girls chase after me because I was a big man. Yeah, *that's* what I wanted, I think. I wanted to be a big man. But, you know, something happened during that first set. I finally didn't care anymore." I felt my throat start to close up. "Because you were over there."

She didn't say anything for a while. Then she said, "I think I'm going to walk home."

And the strange thing was, I just sat there. I didn't

say, "No, I'll drive you, it's too cold and dark to walk," or, "I love you." That would've been the time to say it, right then and there. Just say it and get it over with. Just say, "I don't care about being number one. I don't." But I couldn't say it because I did care. I just sat there on the bench and watched her cut across the lighted parking lot toward her house, and I knew I'd never get another chance to tell her that I loved her.

A COUPLE of weeks after that, an article about Mary Jo came out in the "Sunday Feature Mag" of the Clover Park *Chronicle*. There was a big photo of her holding her racquet and smiling like she'd just hit a winner.

The Sophomore Sensation. That's what the kids at Clover Park High have started calling her. Others have dubbed her "Mt. Mary Jo." She's sixteen, bright, pretty—and just happens to play about the wickedest game of tennis you've ever seen. So wicked that this spring she's shooting for number one on the boys' varsity tennis team.

That's right. Number one . . .

It went on like that. Pure crap.

There's only one person remaining who can keep Mary Jo Mountain from reaching the top. He's the current number one, Roger Otteson, also a sophomore . . .

I think the reporter spelled my last name wrong on purpose. Her name is Meg Cullen-Cozie, and she has this stupid column called "Just Messin' Around," and I can't imagine who reads it because all it's ever about is dumb things her poodle and husband do. Old Meg and that photographer barged into our practice a couple of days after Mary Jo had played her first challenge match, against Russ Redman for number four, and beaten him 6–2, 6–0. That was when people started calling her the Sophomore Sensation. Three days after she beat Redman, she challenged Gary Lim for number two. She beat him 6–1, 6–1. It took her thirty-two minutes. Coach Parks timed it.

Anyway, Meg Cullen-Cozie and this photographer came up and started interviewing Mary Jo and taking pictures of her and all that. I guess they'd been at her house interviewing her family the day before. They talked to Coach Parks for a while, then I saw Coach Parks point in my direction. I was way down at the other end on court 8 with a shopping cart full of tennis balls, hitting serves to Gary Lim. Meg Cullen-Cozie walked up to me and stood off to the side and watched me serve. I acted real cool, you know, like I didn't notice her. I just kept on serving. I hit every serve as hard as I could.

"'Scuse me? Roger?"

I kept up my cool act. I thought of Mike Brock. I tried to picture how he would act in a situation like this.

"How does it feel to be the last one Mary Jo has to beat? What do you think her chances are?"

I thought about hitting another serve before answering Meg Cullen-Cozie's question. That would've been cool. You could picture Brock doing something like that and saying, "Hey, don't rush me, babe. Lemme hit a few more serves."

I lowered my racquet.

"I don't know."

She smiled—probably the same way she smiles at her poodle and husband.

"So, tell me, Roger. What do you think about being challenged for number one by a pretty sixteen-year-old female?"

People had been asking me that since Mary Jo beat Redman. I'd been asking myself since October. I still didn't have an answer.

So I just shrugged and said, "I don't really know."

That was when she asked me how I spelled my last name.

When asked about his chances of withstanding the challenge from the Sophomore Sensation, Roger pauses thoughtfully. He gazes off at Mary Jo, who happens to be hitting a series of flawless two-handed backhands. He stands watching her as though awed, mesmerized. Tall, lanky, curly-haired, he has one of those familiar, I-grew-up-in-Clover-Park faces. He tries to think of a way to answer the question, but words just don't come. Perhaps at night he dreams about Mary Jo Mountain. Perhaps he fears her, idolizes her, hates her. He does not answer the question. How can he? He's never faced a pretty female opponent with an awesome backhand. He doesn't quite know what to make of "Mt. Mary Jo."

What a pile of crap. Now I know why people say you can't believe anything you read in the newspapers.

When the article came out, Mary Jo turned into a celebrity—bigger even than Kortum during football season. The whole week leading up to our match, which was scheduled for Saturday at noon, everybody talked about whether Mary Jo could "do it."

I spent the morning of the match sitting in the family room with my feet on the coffee table, taking deep

169

breaths, trying to get rid of the knot in my stomach. I was all alone. Art was playing golf and Mom had some work to do, but she'd be there for the first serve; she wouldn't miss a single point.

I kept looking up at the clock on the mantel, thinking: I wish this was over.

While I sat there, I went over some of the things that had happened this year—the year I thought would be "my greatest ever." I wondered whether any of it was supposed to add up or fit together somehow, or whether it was just a bunch of stuff that had happened. Why had there been a Paul Mountain and why did his mother have to get a job in Clover Park, and why did he have a twin sister?

I decided that maybe you could never really figure out what the point is to some things. In fact, you were lucky if you could figure out your own self. Especially a guy like me, who couldn't trust himself not to choke in any situation. All year long, things had kept circling around in my head, like, "Too good to be true" and "Give up, you'll always be a Nobody." They had circled around like buzzards.

I looked up at the clock and saw that it was time for me to leave.

24

MARY JO was as nervous as I was. I could tell by the way she smiled at me and said "Hi" and reached out to take the three brand-new yellow tennis balls that Coach Parks handed her.

We started warming up. Cars were pulling into the parking lot, doors were slamming, people were finding places to sit on the bleachers or on the grassy hillside.

In the top row of the bleachers, Mom was leaning forward and talking to somebody a couple rows in front of her. It was Marc Mountain, Mary Jo's dad. Mom had on her salesperson's smile. After all, she had sold the guy a house.

When we had finished warming up, Coach Parks took Mary Jo's racquet and spun it. Since I was the one being challenged, I had the choice of calling up or down. I called up, and it was up. I decided to serve first. Attack the net, hold serve, get some confidence right away.

At the baseline, I held up two tennis balls in my left

hand to signal that I was ready to start the match. I put one ball in my pocket and bounced the other a few times.

Everything became quiet. I could feel my heart pumping. It made me think of that day, way back in the fall, when I had walked up to the practice field, thumping my football helmet against my thigh pad. Thump, thump, thump. 66 Day had seemed a long way off then. I had all the hope in the world.

Mary Jo got down in her ready position, swaying just a bit.

I caressed the ball in my fingertips and tossed it. It seemed to pause in midair, a round yellow ball against the blue sky, and for a second it reminded me of the way the football had hung in the sky against the bright lights in Clover Park Stadium, and how I had to decide whether or not to call for a fair catch.

My strings moved across the ball as I let out an *Uhmph.*

I sat down on the bench and realized that five games had gone by. Five games, just like that.

A scoreboard was hanging on the chain-link fence at one end of the court. I looked at it.

MOUNTAIN	OTTOSEN
4	1

Mary Jo was a few feet away from me, bending down to pull up her short girl-socks. She straightened up, toweled off the grip of her racquet, and took a deep, satisfied breath. She was making all her shots—angles, lobs, passing shots. I wasn't concentrating, wasn't staying on my toes, wasn't hitting the ball smoothly or following through or getting lucky. I wasn't doing anything.

She served to start game number six. I attacked the ball, telling myself I had to be more aggressive. When I rushed the net, she put up a lob—for once it wasn't a perfect one. It peaked and started toward me. I watched the seams revolving. Racquet cocked, left arm pointing at the ball, I arched my back and brought my racquet overhead with all my weight behind it. I smashed it. The ball bounced in her court and took a high hop over the fence. The crowd laughed and applauded. Some kid had to run out to the parking lot to get it as it rolled under parked cars on its way to the street.

It was a good shot.

I fought my way back to 3–4. During our change of sides, I crouched over with my hands on my knees and tried to think. Mary Jo would be serving this game with a 4–3 lead. It would be good if I could break her serve here and tie up the set, then hold my serve and take a 5–4 lead. That would be a nice turnaround.

But I didn't break her serve. The set score went to 3–5. Then my own serve fell apart in the ninth game, and the first set was history, 3–6.

The crowd shouted and whistled as we walked to the bench. The sun was starting to heat up the court. I picked up my plastic water bottle and squirted some water into my mouth. I could feel it run all the way down to my stomach. I thought of the cold bottle of Gatorade waiting for me at home in the refrigerator. But I knew it wasn't good to think about things like that. The less thinking, the better.

The first three games of the second set went to deuce. Back and forth, deuce, ad, deuce, ad. The court got hotter and hotter and I felt like I was slowly getting cooked. My concentration kept getting broken by all kinds of weird thoughts that darted in and out of my mind. I kept losing track of the score and a couple of times I started to serve in the wrong court.

Somewhere in the third game, I noticed the two kids. Between points, I kept looking up at them. They were standing at the top of the hill, watching the match and smoking cigarettes. One cigarette after another. Mr. Phillips, a math teacher, went up there with a slip of paper and took down their names. The two kids walked off across the field, shaking their heads and spitting, their hands dug deep in the front pockets of their jeans.

As the third game went on and on—deuce, ad, deuce, ad, deuce—I wondered what Mr. Phillips was going to do with that slip of paper. Probably give it to the vice principal on Monday. The VP would call the two kids into his office, one at a time, and give them a lecture and detention after school.

The crowd was applauding. I had just lost the third game of the second set. In fact, I had lost the first three games.

I glanced at the scoreboard to remind myself that I was down 0–3 in the second set and there'd be no third set if I lost this one.

That's when I started to panic.

I walked out to the baseline to serve the fourth game. A few polite people clapped for me. I cupped the ball lightly in three fingers as I got ready to serve. The toss went up, nice and smooth. I could feel my strings skip across the ball and make it spin. I grunted—*Uumph*—and followed through. Net. I tried again. *Aaooomph.*

I was halfway to the net before I realized I'd double-faulted.

• • •

Sitting on the bench again, I squinted at the scoreboard, barely able to read it because of the glare of the sun and the sweat running down into my eyes.

MOUNTAIN	OTTOSEN
4	1

How many times in my life had I come back from 1–4? Lots. There was that semifinal match against Gunderson last year. And that time against...

I pictured that bottle of Gatorade waiting for me at home, and it looked awfully good.

The crowd clapped for Mary Jo as she walked briskly out to the baseline. She looked as if she was telling herself, Put him away.

But I was already put away. I didn't want to get up and go back out there and serve, but I had to.

As I trudged out to the baseline, I noticed a man in a yellow sweater and brown golf hat, standing on the other side of the chain-link fence. Art's face looked hard and leathery.

I wanted to tell him, One of us has to lose, Art.

It took me such a long time to walk out to the baseline that some of the people in the crowd started to get restless and noisy. "Go get him, Mary Jo!" they were yelling. "Do it, Mary Jo!"

I took a deep breath. I bounced the ball a few times, waiting for things to quiet down a little, even though I wasn't really thinking about getting my concentration back. At 1–4 in the second set, it was a little late to be thinking about anything at all. It would be best just to get it over with as quickly and painlessly as possible.

The yelling got louder. Coach Parks stood up and started moving his hands in a downward motion. I lowered my racquet and took a couple of steps away from the baseline. I could feel Art behind me, watching me. He probably had the same look on his face that he'd had the night he tied my necktie for me; the same one when he held up his wineglass and said, "Give 'em hell out there."

I turned around and looked at Art. He was looking back at me. Then, just barely, he smiled and gave a single nod.

I stepped back to the baseline and looked across the net at Mary Jo. I asked myself a simple question: Should I even bother anymore?

I still hadn't answered it as I served and charged the net. The ball took a high hop to her backhand. She cocked her racquet and fired the ball down the line on my forehand side. The next thing I knew, I was diving through the air. I felt my racquet meet the ball and punch it, and as I skidded across the pavement and came to a stop, I heard the crowd burst into applause. It wasn't until I stood up that I realized they were clapping because I'd made the shot.

I didn't bother aiming my next serve, I just threw my whole body behind it and followed it to the net. Even before she hit the return, I could sense she was going to try to pass me on my forehand side again. This time I didn't have to dive; I was right on top of the ball and volleyed it away for a winner. 30–love.

Next point, I rushed the net again, found myself stretched out horizontally in midair, and volleyed the ball crosscourt as I came down on my right hip. 40–love.

I called time out and limped over to the sideline, where Mr. Parks handed me a clean white towel. Blood was running down my right knee and soaking my sock.

There was a big scrape on my elbow. I could hear the crowd murmuring. The strawberry on my right hip stung. But it wasn't a bad kind of pain, it was like running the bluff, that kind of pain. Not the kind that eats away at your stomach, like when you see some unobtainable girl walking down the hall.

At 40–love, Mary Jo tried to pass me on my backhand, but the ball went wide. The scoreboard changed to 4–2.

I broke her serve, then held mine. The set score went to 4–4. As Mary Jo started serving the ninth game, I could tell she was tightening up. At 30–all, she double-faulted. It was break point, 30–40. If I could break her serve here, I'd be up 5–4 and serving for the second set.

She stayed on the baseline, working me from side to side, daring me to come to the net. When she hit a drop shot, it took me totally by surprise. I sprinted in on it and scooped the ball over the net. Mary Jo was waiting. She planted her feet and drilled the ball so hard it looked like a rifle shot. Right at my face. All I could do was lift my racquet. I felt my eyes go cross-eyed as the ball hit my strings and ricocheted over the net at a sharp angle, out of Mary Jo's reach.

I had broken her serve. People were standing and applauding for both of us as we walked to the sideline to change sides.

Mary Jo sat down on the bench and buried her face in a towel. I knew what she was thinking. She was saying to herself, "He's too hot. Save yourself for the third set. Damn," she was saying, "damn, damn, damn. Save everything you've got for the third set."

I won the second set, 6–4. I was glad we weren't

177

changing sides. I'd have had too much time to pat myself on the back. I'd be sitting there congratulating myself on my comeback, while Mary Jo would be mentally erasing the second set and getting ready for the third and final one.

25

THE THIRD SET had been going on for over an hour. The court was now covered with shadows. Mary Jo and I had been dead-even the whole set, right up to this twelfth game. There hadn't been a single service break. Every point had been a battle.

Mary Jo was serving at 5–6, 30–all. I was two points away from winning the match; she was two points away from taking it to a tiebreaker.

We started a long rally. As I rushed the net, she passed me cleanly on my forehand side. The ball landed wide by a few inches. Out. Mary Jo grimaced to the sky, like she'd just been shot.

Match point.

Her first serve smacked into the net. I wiped the sweat off my grip with my shirttail.

Her second serve was cautious. The rally began. I stayed back, waiting for the right time to come to the net. She kept her shots up the middle, not daring to aim for the corners.

One of her forehands landed shallow. I played it and continued up to the net. She fired one right up the middle that slapped the top of the net and bounced at my feet. I sent the ball back, high and deep, and she responded with a lob. I backpedaled, kicked my left leg into the air, and smashed the ball. She got her racquet on it and put up another shaky lob. I waited, watched the ball spin toward me, and smashed it again. It bounced into her court and shot past her. The match was over.

The crowd applauded as I waited for Mary Jo at the net. She came toward me, her face blank. We shook hands. She didn't say anything, although she met my eyes briefly before she turned and walked toward the bench.

I stayed where I was, my hands resting on the net. I watched Mary Jo gather up her racquets, warm-ups, and towel. People started to surround her. As she walked off the court, she turned and gave me one last look over her shoulder.

Then everybody closed in on me. Coach Parks congratulated me. Mom hugged me. Art reached out to shake my hand. His hand was hard and leathery, like his face. I held on to it tightly.

Later, I was back in the family room, with my Gatorade. Mom was at work and Art had gone to finish his eighteen holes, so I was alone. The house was dead quiet.

It wasn't bad being alone. The weird part was that six hours before, I had been sitting there, wearing the same clothes and everything, looking at that picture of Mary Jo in the Clover Park *Chronicle*, and moaning, "Just let it be over."

And now it was over.

The phone rang. I pulled myself off the couch and

felt my bones crack and creak as I walked over to answer it, carrying my Gatorade with me.

"Hey, ugly."

It was Brodie. I smiled.

"I was there today," he said. "Would you believe that?"

"No. I didn't see you."

"Well, I was there."

"How'd I look?" I asked.

"Ugly as usual. But I managed to stay awake."

"Thanks," I said. "What are you doing tonight?" My grip around the phone tightened. "You want to go bowling? It's Red Pin Nite."

He couldn't. He had a date.

I pumped him for the details before I hung up. It was quiet again. I took a swig of Gatorade. Brodie on a date, what do you know? I stood staring at the phone and wondered about Mary Jo. I thought of that last look she had given me over her shoulder, so sad and final.

The sound of the doorbell made me jump.

It rang again as I hurried through the kitchen. I opened the front door.

It was Mary Jo. She hadn't changed out of her tennis warm-ups.

"Hi," I said quietly.

"Hi."

We stood there for an awkward moment. Then she said something about buying me a Coke. She'd drive.

I hurried back to the family room, grabbed my keys, and locked the front door. She opened the passenger door for me and I climbed in.

"Well," she said, looking over her shoulder as she backed out of the driveway, "I'm glad it's over."

"Yeah."

I knew it would never be over. She'd be able to re-challenge me midway through the season; football turn-outs would be starting up in August; another 66 Day; then another tennis season. I looked over at her, about to tell her what I was thinking, when I realized what it must have taken for her to walk up to my front door and ring the bell.

So, instead of saying anything, I rolled down the window, leaned back, and let the fresh cool wind rush in against my face.